I0762246

JANICE'S ENTANGLEMENT

THE RATHE CHRONICLES BOOK 2

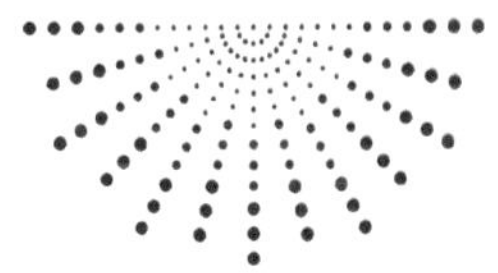

ALEXANDRA K. MARTIN

Second Edition 2022,

Ebook: 978-0-6450508-6-8

Paperback: 978-0-6453856-1-8

Hardback: 978-0-6453856-4-9

Cover and Title Art © DAZED Designs 2021

Editor: Insomniac Editing Services

Proofreader: Melissa Plant

Formatter: © DAZED Designs 2021

"The most difficult thing is the decision to act, the rest is merely tenacity."

— AMELIA EARHART

FOREWARNING

Please be aware that I'm an Australian writer, therefore this book is written with British spelling in mind.

This is also a Fantasy/PNR Menage novel, with adult content and is recommended for the mature audience. It may contain some darker elements such as violence and drowning, please keep this warning in mind going forward.

Enter at your own risk...

*Insert evil laugh

To my husband PT and my wife Jen. Without your love, support, laughter, and lack of censorship I would go mad.
Thanks for always loving me just the way I am and putting up with my crazy shenanigans.
Love your ass.
Love your tits.

GLOSSARY

KINDREDS & KIDS

Summer

Blayze (Phoenix)

Salvatore (Dragon)

Reid (Alpha Wolf)

Baine (Omega Wolf)

Kids

- Meaghan (Human Female)
- Lawson (Human Male)

- Llewellyn (Human Female, Twin set A - Identical)
- Cheyenne (Human Female, Twin set A - Identical)
- Mina (Phoenix Female, Twin set B)
- Demetrius (Dragon Male, Twin set B)

MHANU

Shifters

Phoenix (Rare and Powerful/ most feared shifter)
Dragons

- Dragon (fire Dragon/most powerful)
- Leviathan (Water Dragon)
- Drake (Earth Dragon/ no wings)

Wolf
Grizzly Bear
Shark
Cheetah

Sorcerers

Fae

Elves (Earth)
Fairy (Air)
Siren (Water)
Wielders (Fire)

Downworlders

Vampyre
Demon

DIVINE ORDER

Guardians

Angel
Valkyrie

Celestials

Catholic/Christian God (In charge of Angel)
Norse Gods (In charge of Valkyrie)
Azraelle (Goddess of Rebirth)

PLACES

Rathe (Parallel world to Earth)

Threshold (Holding facility for human woman stolen by Rathe for reproductive purposes)

Downworld (World of darkness below and connected to both worlds)

Bermuda Triangle (Door between both worlds)

PROLOGUE

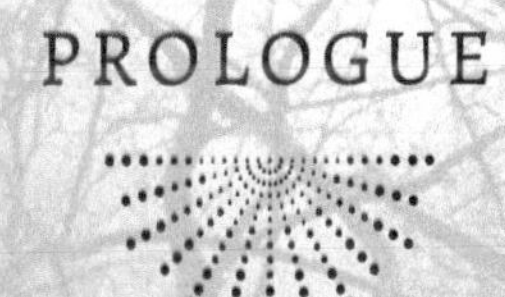

Janice

The girls and I sit here flinching as we hear yet another scream coming from the Alpha lodges. It's been a long day and Summer's been a trooper trying to get out that baby. I can't wait to see what it is but it sucks that there's no epidural here.

There's a sudden silence followed by a resounding *Whoop*!

Reid comes running to the centre and calls out proudly to his pack. "We have a Dragon son! He's big and healthy, and Summer's amazing. A boy is born!"

Around us men change to animals and they howl and growl their victory into the world, and it once warms my heart to hear such joy, regardless of the species of child that's born. These people come together and rejoice in the birth of an innocent child, in a way that humans never do.

The appreciation of life regardless of gender or species is one of pure bliss and I feel so honoured to be a part of it.

One day this will be me and I'll gladly take it.

Today there are species other than the Wolves and the Alphas present. I see Tigers, Grizzly Bears, Eagles, and Owls. It's quite incredible.

"*Aaaaaahh!*" Another unexpected scream wrenches through the air and Reid goes white before racing back to his Kindred at warp speed.

More fierce screams follow and my stomach drops. What's happening? *No*. Fear fills me and I think of the worst.

Bell is up and racing towards the lodge in seconds, fear written all over her face and Havana and I look at each other with worry.

"She has to be ok," I try to lighten the mood. "She's too stubborn not to be."

Her kids walk over to us looking confused. "What's happening?" Summers' son, Lawson, asks nervously, gazing back towards the lodge.

I smile at him. "I'm not sure, sweety. Your mum is just finishing up. How exciting that you have a brother now, you must be glad since you have so many sisters?"

He nods but still stares off when another terrifying scream is let loose and then complete silence. "Mum?" He whispers with tears brimming his eyes.

Llewellyn comes and sits on my lap, her eyes wide and scared. "It's okay, darling, this is normal," I say reassuringly, stroking her hair softly but I look over to Havana's terrified face, my heart feels just as petrified as her expression.

Almighty roars come from the lodge before Baine comes barreling through the trees, tears pouring down his cheeks.

"A Phoenix rises again. A girl! We have a daughter and a son."

The crowd goes wild, animals and men alike. A breath I didn't know I was holding blows out of my lungs in utter relief.

Baine comes over and picks up Cheyenne, giving her a kiss on the cheek. "Did you hear that, guys? Mama had more twins, a boy and a girl."

"What's their name, Papa? Is Mummy alright?" Meaghan asks, relief washing her tear-stained face.

Smiling at the kids like the proud Dad he is, Baine states, "Aye, your Mama did so well." Stroking Llewellyn's little face with love as she stands by him. "Demetrius and Mina are their names, and they're perfect. Come and see them, guys." Reaching his hand out for them and bouncing Cheyenne on his hip.

I know he includes us but I quietly decline because I want them to enjoy their special family time. I'm so happy for them, this is such a special day for everyone.

They all walk off happily, laughing with each other, and I silently slip away to the girl's lodge, where I stay.

Opening my door, I walk inside, it takes me a minute before I realise that the door took a longer time than usual to close and I turn around to see a large bald man with arms as thick as tree trunks leaning against my door, staring at me with dark sinister eyes. I know instantly that I'm in danger.

Before I can even scream something knocks me hard in the back of my head and everything goes black...

CHAPTER ONE

"Janice!" Somebody shakes me awake. "Janice!" I groan, swatting away the offending hand.

"Guys, leave me alone. I have a headache." I don't want to deal with another one of my brother's crazy schemes that I just *know* he'll drag me into. "Tell Ma I'm coming. Sheesh." My head's pounding hard in rhythm with my heart as I moan.

A quiet husky girl's voice says, "Janice, it's Havana. You have to wake up. Please." *Wait, what?* I sit straight up. Huge mistake! The pain just intensifies and my stomach instantly wants to evacuate.

"Argh," I whine tiredly. I try to rub the back of my head but my hands are restrained for some reason.

Slowly opening my eyes, I look to my hands in front of me and see that my wrists are tied together by a rope. Turning my head carefully, because it and my neck are really feeling subpar right now, I take in my surroundings.

I'm sitting in the woods on the rough ground next to my friend Havana and two other girls, I recognise one from Threshold. Alice,

I think her name is, a shorter girl on the bigger side. Something about her always seemed so melancholy. The other girl is about my age, with smooth dark skin, great cheekbones, and a beautiful full head of bouncy hair. This girl is blessed.

Havana and I became really close since living together with Reid's pack. She's a quiet girl, and only really talks to me and the other girls who live there, Summer and Bell. "Sweety, why are we out here? And why am I tied up?" My voice is soft as I ask Havana. I look around at the endless trees encapsulating us, breathe in the fresh earthy scent that blows over me, and caresses my face.

Havana just shakes her head, fear filling her eyes, before she looks at her own bound hands, clearly affected by what's happening and unable to voice it.

"We were taken by the Six Pack." Alice fills in for Havana, leaning towards me. "We heard them say something about selling us at a market or something odd like that."

Geez, that doesn't seem good. I'm not worried though, Reid's pack will find us. I decide to smile at Alice instead of freaking out, "How have you been, Alice? I haven't seen you in a hot minute." She just shrugs sadly, looking as if her whole world's coming to an end. Her big eyes are deep and filled with an emotion that I could never pretend to comprehend. "I wouldn't worry about it too much, our pack will be here shortly. I have no doubt about that. They can be a pain in the behind, but they're family now." I try to lift their spirits a bit by sharing some of my unyielding faith in my new unorthodox family.

Alice and the other girl look at each other in silence before looking back at me.

"Um... While I appreciate your faith, I don't think anyone's coming. You've been out for a day already, they must've hit you pretty hard." The unknown girl says in an English accent. "The Six Pack means business, love. They're a pretty scary bunch too." She fidgets where she sits, looking acutely uncomfortable telling me this. Her gaze flits around to see if anyone can hear her.

"What are they?" Havana almost whispers, her whole body tensing next to me.

"Grizzly Bears," Alice replies. "Big ones. I thought they were going to eat us at first." Her big eyes fill with unshed tears.

"Now, now. None of that ladies, if we stick together, we can accomplish anything. Girl power and all that." I attempt to lighten the mood, pointedly ignoring my still steady headache.

"Well, well, well. The princess has arisen." A deep baritone voice pronounces, with an obvious mocking undertone. "Good, because it's time we get going. Boys, let's head out."

I get to my knees and turn my body around to see six large men behind our tree, packing up some random things that are laying around and stuffing them into bags. One of them is the big bald guy that I remember leaning against my door before I was knocked out. His eyes lock with mine for a moment before he smirks and keeps on packing. *Rude much?*

Standing myself up off the dirt, I help the others to their feet too, the best that I can with tied wrists anyway. I dust myself off a bit and raise my hands in front of me.

"Excuse me, gentleman, but would it be possible for you to untie the ladies and myself. This really isn't necessary." I use my polite voice, I'm sure we can all be reasonable here.

The blond Bear shifter closest to us, who's missing an ear, turns around and scoffs, "No can do, pet. Now just close that pretty mouth of yours and do as you're told, or I'll be giving it another use." His salacious look turns my stomach and shocks me. *Why I never!*

"Excuse me?" I reply, my jaw dropping at his crassness.

"You're gonna need to open it wider than that to accommodate me, pet," he drops his stuff on the ground and stalks towards me with evident purpose.

I involuntarily step back, "Why you're nothing but bad news. Your point has been made, sir, no need to come further." I shudder at the thought. Disgusting.

Son of a gun, I hope that the Alphas don't take too long, I don't think these guys are messing around. After rounding up their stuff, two very similar looking Bear shifters thread our wrist restraints with a long rope, connecting us together, then hands us over to another man who proceeds to pull us through the woods.

It's a nice enough trek they take us on, endless tall trees, a nice breeze, and delicate wildflowers along the untamed ground, but they're moving at such a fast pace that poor Alice is struggling. We walk for hours, only stopping for the odd toilet and water break. The only thing to snack on is the beef jerky that they randomly hand to us. It's not much but I'll take it.

I eventually find out the other girl is Nateesha; she's pleasant enough, not very talkative, but nice regardless. Apparently, Alice and Nateesha were together with a herd of male Stag shifter, Nateesha claims that they're a nice group, but they don't hold out any hope of them coming after them because they're considerably lower on the food chain compared to the Grizzly's dragging us through the wild.

After half of the day with no further conversation, I just can't stand it anymore, so I decide to pep everyone up and to get to know everybody a little bit better. "So where are y'all from anyway? I'm from Kansas in the US of A, and Havana here's from New Zealand, right sweety?" I prompt and Havana just nods in agreement, choosing not to contribute past there, but that's not abnormal for her.

"Ah, well, I'm from just outside London, in the UK. I've never been anywhere else until now," Nateesha replies, although somewhat reluctantly.

I peer at Alice expectantly, who sighs, "Seattle." Obviously, she's not keen to converse but it doesn't deter me.

I clap my hands excitedly, "That's great. Before all of this Rathe business, I was living on my Ma and Pa's ranch with two of my brothers. Two of the others have a little place together in town, and my oldest brother lives with his wife and my three nephews. They all still work on the ranch though, it's the family business and all that. I helped out a little in the past, but I'd just finished college and was about to get into the paperwork side of the business. You know the guys just didn't have a head for that sort of thing, bless their hearts." I always find myself smiling when thinking about my family, my brothers drive me crazy sometimes, but I love them.

"Does that mean you've five brothers?" Nateesha asks wide-eyed.

I nod enthusiastically, "You betcha. I'm the baby of the family, so you can just imagine what it was like trying to bring a suitor home, poor things never stood a chance. My Ma was determined to get herself a girl, which is why there's so many of us. She was so happy to have me that I was showered with everything pink and frilly. I had to do beauty pageants, singing lessons, and I've always been a cheerleader. I loved it though. It's always fun doing all the pretty things." I suddenly stop to take in a breath and laugh hard, "My Pa though, he said that I was one of his and as such, I would carry his name proudly. He taught me how to shoot my first gun when I was just four years old. I'm a better shot than my good for nothing brothers, they're terrible hunters. Don't get confused though, that lot of grubs are my best friends, they've always been there for me, mostly driving me up the wall and trying to get me into trouble from their ridiculous stunts. My life was always good when I wasn't at the receiving end of my brother's pranks. I went hunting, camping, and fishing with my Pa and the boys regularly, he said no daughter of his would be useless. Poor Ma, she just wanted one clean child, but I was just as covered in mud as the boys were."

The rope suddenly tugs hard and almost has me landing on my face. If it wasn't for all those years of cheerleading, I would have. My reflexes were solid. "What on God's green Earth was that for?" I ask the surly-looking Bear shifter holding the rope.

"We're not on Earth, pet, now shut the fuck up." He fires back.

"Do *not* use that kind of language on me, Sir, thank you very much. If you don't like what I'm saying then just don't listen." I stop to pop my hip out and raise one of my eyebrows at him with attitude.

"Female, if you don't shut your mouth I'm gonna shut it for you!" He sneers, before pulling hard on the rope again to get us moving.

This time Alice falls over and lands hard on her knees before being dragged a bit by the awful shifter man. She begins to cry while trying to get back onto her knees, which is useless with bound hands.

"Stop!" I cry out, "You're hurting her." The girls and myself scramble to grab Alice before any bad damage is done to her.

"Bruce, I'll take over. Give your ears a rest, my friend." The bald man from my lodge comes over and laughs heartily at the scene before him.

Bruce hands over the rope with a, "*Thank fuck*" and storms off to join the others at the front.

Bald lodge guy turns to us, his face now as hard as granite, obviously to get his point across that he's not playing with us, "You have two minutes to get yourselves together before we move. Hurry up." At least he's giving us a moment to help Alice.

"Thank you so much, Mr?" I ask, clearly waiting for a response.

His cold stare answering me. I smile back at his stoic face, "Now, I know you have a name, it seems like we're gonna be in each other's company for a while, so names seem like the least we should know. I'm Janice, nice to meet you."

"I'm not here to be your friend, Janice." He blandly responds, but I just keep smiling patiently, unaffected by his coldness, while the other girls help Alice out. He'll break, eventually, they always do.

He huffs out his frustration, "Anton." A simple statement. "Times up." He says before he turns, pulling us forward again. Score one to Janice, I think to myself while stifling a laugh.

"Pleasure to meet you, Anton," My voice is filled with sugar as I turn to the girls, who are now looking at me quizzically. They're obviously confused about why I'm being nice to our so-called enemies.

My Da always said, "Play smart, not hard." But my Ma was the one who taught me to kill them with kindness. Between the two of them, I can't go wrong.

"So where was I?" I continue like nothing happened. "Oh right, Kansas life. Well, we got an awful lot more tornadoes than I would've liked there being, but we're a God-fearing lot and know how to appreciate what we have, while we have it. Across the road from me was the most beautiful sunflower field you've ever seen. I just love sunflowers, don't you? There's nothing happier than a bright and beautiful thing that follows the sunshine all day." I feel nostalgic even thinking about it, warmth filling my heart, remembering the flower's smell blowing in the wind.

"You know there's more than one God right?" I hear come from Anton as he continues facing forward and walking.

"That's nice," I just brush off his unwanted intrusion.

"Anywho, some of my favourite memories are of when I was a teenager, we used to sneak out to the fields in the middle of the night to drink cheap beer and look up at the stars. The best nights were when the lightning bugs were out in force, flickering away and dancing to the sound of the night. It's the simple things, you know? I do miss it there." I sigh deeply at the memory of home.

I keep talking all afternoon, no one else has much to say today, but that's okay, I like to talk, and it always cheers people up. There's nothing better than sharing a story amongst friends and I can clearly see that they're much more relaxed than they were in the contemplative silence.

We finally get to a clearing as the day starts to set, the warm heat of the sun disappearing over the horizon of the mountains before us, and we're placed down and told not to move. There's a pretty little river to the right of us; I concentrate on not overthinking things, and just sit back to enjoy the priceless view.

CHAPTER TWO

Two of the guys, Anton and the big blond guy with an ear missing, stay behind with us as the others go off in different directions. I'm assuming it's to hunt or check the perimeter.

Anton comes over with a huge rock, puts it down in front of our semi-circle, plonking his bottom onto it, and looks at us one at a time, but I feel like he lingers on me longer than necessary. He's actually pretty good looking for someone so hard, and clearly awful. Not traditionally handsome though, but he has a dark, sexy aura going on instead. He reminds me of a taller version of Vin Diesel, with a lot of scary being put out, but it works for him, and his baritone voice rattles my bones when he speaks, it's so low and deep.

"Right, it's time to update the newcomers," he starts, "we're the Six Pack..." I cut him off with a snicker. His eyes shoot to me, "Is something amusing you, pet?"

I smile back sweetly, "It's just... Six Pack? What, like beer? Do you come in heavy or light?" I hear Nateesha cough-laugh before covering it up quickly.

He scowls at me, "I assure you, we only come in heavy."

At that, I do laugh... out loud. I can't help it, I laugh so hard my cheeks hurt. I hear the other Bear shifter growling angrily and I try to contain myself, and mostly succeed.

I look up and see the humour in Anton's eyes before he covers it with his usual stoic expression. Who knew he had a sense of humour, maybe he isn't so bad after all.

"As I was saying before I was so rudely interrupted," Anton looks at me pointedly, "we're Bears for hire, it's our job, and today you're our merchandise. Lucky you. We've been directed not to kill you or affect your breeding capabilities in any way, but other than that we have free reign. If you try to run away or disrespect us in any form we have no problem removing a tongue or a leg, you don't need those to reproduce and that's all you're good for here." Anton states blatantly, "The best outcome you can hope to have is to behave well enough that you're bought by someone that takes care of his livestock. A maimed female will fetch a lower price, and therefore will go to someone more desperate and less likely to be encouraged toward long term health or care. You have been warned."

With that, he gets up and walks over to the other guys, and they chuckle quietly amongst themselves. Apparently, he *is* that bad. Apprehension fills me with how serious this suddenly feels.

A sob is torn from Havana and I turn to see both her and Alice crying quietly, huddled together. Nateesha just looks shocked and scared, mouth and eyes wide open.

"It'll be alright, the Alphas will catch up to us tonight, Havana. You'll see." I reassuringly squeeze her hand with mine, while trying desperately to believe what I'm saying, a smile still dawning my face. I refuse to let these males bring me down.

After we have some rabbit that they caught for dinner, I get up off the ground and walk over to Anton who's looking out over the river.

I clear my throat to get his attention. "What do you want, Janice?" He barks out, without even turning around.

"Hey, how did you know it was me?"

"You all have a different scent, I'm sure you've figured that out by now. What do you want?"

"What do I smell like? What is a Janice smell?" I wonder out loud.

He turns slowly in my direction, with both eyebrows raised. "Seriously?"

I nod, smiling. He puts his chin to his chest and shakes his head in exasperation. "You're so frustrating. What... Do... You... Want?" He pronounces each word firmly as he looks back up at me with narrowed eyes.

At this point, I can see that he's getting angry with me, so I get to the point. "May I please go to the ladies room, and how far away do we have left to travel?"

He purses his lips in thought, "Tomorrow we have one more village to stop at and pick up some merchandise from, and then another three days walk to our destination." He squints his eyes, "What's a ladies room?"

I feel myself going a little red. "Um, I need to empty my bladder."

"Ah. Hold on." Turning to face the guys he calls out to the blond one from earlier, "Nemo, I'm taking this female to urinate."

I scrunch up my face and cross my arms. "Did you have to yell it like that?"

"Yep." He walks up the side of the river, away from where I'm standing, going past the clearing. "Are you coming? Or are you going to do it there?" He shouts back as he starts to disappear through the trees next to the water.

It's early enough that the sun hasn't quite gone down yet so we can still see clearly. I shuffle over to catch up to him, "Sorry."

We walk for a little while and then he stops before a big rock next to the river, turning to me he undoes my binds. "You can go behind that." Pointing to the boulder. "If you need to you can wash yourself off in the water after, you're getting a bit stinky for my liking."

I look down at my skirt and leather sandals. "I'd get my underclothes wet if I did that because I've got no towel."

"Use your panties to dry yourself and go without." He says in a matter of fact way. "Or just don't clean yourself and smell like that. Your choice."

I sigh heavily. They're getting kinda yucky from the trek and I wish I had more to wear. Maybe I can wash them, then leave them to dry overnight, my skirt goes past my knees so I could probably get away with it. I walk over to the rock, remove my shoes and underwear, placing them to the side, before doing my business. I then tread into the water, it's a beautiful temperature and I immediately feel relieved as the lukewarm water swirls around my feet and legs as I wade further in.

I start lifting my skirt higher, with the intention of going waist deep and giving myself a little clean. I look over and see that Anton is watching my every move.

"Do you mind? I'm gonna wash up a bit." Figuring that he's just waiting for confirmation.

"I don't mind at all." He sits down on the stony shore, leaning on his hands with his legs stretched out in front of him, a mischievous smile lining his usually tight features, "By all means, continue. You might as well take it all off and get a really good wash."

I gawk at him in astonishment, he's just going to sit there watching me. I turn and go further away, but am stopped by Anton's command, "That's far enough or I'll come in there and get you."

I pull my skirt up as high as I can without showing any of my vitals, while facing away from him, and I carefully clean myself. I hear a deep rumbling behind me and look over my shoulder to see Anton on one knee leaning forward with a hand braced on the ground like he's going to pounce in my direction at any moment. I stop washing myself immediately and slowly make my way out of the river, lowering my skirt as I go. The heat I see in his eyes leaves me feeling more than a little frazzled and he watches my every move, reminding me that he's the predator and I am merely the prey.

Walking to the shore, the smooth stones beneath my toes, I head towards my stuff, giving him my back and trying to slow my racing heart.

"You should be very careful about what you do in front of the males in Rathe, you've been here long enough to know better." Anton rumbles from right behind me as I bend over to pick up my shoes. I can feel his body heat behind me because he's so close and I slowly rise back up, making no sudden movements as I do.

"I'm done now," I say breathlessly, my chest rising and falling heavily with our close vicinity. "I just can't find my underclothes, they were here before."

"Sadly they were tossed away with the breeze," he whispers near my ear. I'm so stupid. Of course, he threw them away, I shouldn't have trusted him, I just wanted to be clean.

Turning around to look up at him, I see heat and desire in his eyes, "I'm... Um... I'm ready to go now." I stammer out, deciding against fighting over where my panties are.

Anton leans forward and breathes me in deeply with his eyes closed. "Honey and sunshine," he says simply.

"What?" I'm confused.

"That's what your scent is." He leans into the nape of my neck inhaling and rubs his nose up my sensitive skin. My body responds to his closeness, goosebumps shiver over my flesh and I gasp at the light but deliberate touch. The way he breathes me in, the way his eyes heat up, his leathery smell surrounding me, it all pulls me in and for a moment I'm lost. I wish I had those panties right about now.

All of a sudden he grabs a handful of my hair and yanks me ahead of him with a, "Move it. You've taken long enough." Now I'm even more confused, and a bit angry at my body for getting all hot and bothered over this big Bear-man. Traitorous body.

I walk ahead and just before I get to the girls, Anton grabs my arm so I have to turn and look at him. He holds up the rope for my hands, I comply and put my hands up for him but he shakes his head and goes behind me, taking my wrists with him.

"What are you doing? I need them in the front." Feeling a bit panicked as he ties them up behind my back.

With me faced towards the river, away from everyone, he leans down over my shoulder and says quietly, "Now it's easier to see these." And he reaches around, pinching my nipples so hard that I yelp and my traitorous body once again defies me as they pebble taught and ask for more. "Hmm, now your honey smells even sweeter than before. Delicious." Nibbling on my ear lobe, "Be careful you don't drip, pet." He stalks off, leaving me panting and frustrated. How dare he do that to me and how dare my body celebrate it!

I try to catch my breath to calm my nipples back down, while I squeeze my legs together. *Get control of yourself, Janice.* Walking back over to the girls I plunk myself down with a pout.

"Why are your hands behind your back now?" Nateesha looks at me curiously.

I roll my eyes dramatically and nudge my head in the direction of the Bear-men. "Anton thinks he's funny."

She gives me a sympathetic smile, "That's going to make things a lot harder for you."

"Yep, I suppose it will. Oh well, I'll manage." I smile at the girls to show them I'm fine. "My brothers have done worse to me than this in the past, these guys are amateurs compared to those boys. They're just a bit too big for their britches is all." I lay down and wiggle myself into a comfy spot, at least as comfortable as I can be considering how I'm tied up.

With that, we settle down for the night, huddling together for comfort and warmth. It's not the best night sleep of my life, but a whole lot better than that hell night we endured back at Threshold. Even thinking about it gives me the willies.

CHAPTER THREE

I wake up to hands tugging on my shirt, pulling it up to my chest. *What the heck?*

Looking up I see one of those blasted Bear-men handling me. "Get your filthy hands off of my shirt!" I crow out in outrage.

It's the grumpy one that was dragging us along earlier, he covers my mouth with his hand and yanks my shirt up to my neck with his other. *Oh my gosh!*

"Stop! What are you doing to her?" I hear Alice call out and I see her sit up and try to pull my shirt back down.

Slap!

The Bear-man backhands her right in the mouth, knocking her back with a whimper. I bite his hand as hard as I can and kick up with my foot, connecting with the side of his head. Hard. That's right buddy, don't mess with a cheerleader!

"Fucking bitch!" He roars, holding the side of his head and giving me momentary space to roll out from under him and away. I use my tumbling experience and pop up onto my feet in a heartbeat, I need to be standing if I have a chance against this giant. Alice huddles over with Nateesha and Havana, crying and holding her face. Bear-man turns to them with malice, so I kick a rock in his direction, getting him in the leg.

Turning back to me, I say to him, with my eyes narrowed, "You wanted to touch me, well here's your chance." There's no way I'm letting him hurt those girls anymore, I'd rather take the beating myself.

"You little whore. You need to learn your place, get on your knees where you belong!" He snaps at me, striding towards me with hard, angry steps.

As he reaches me I drop to my knees with a sweet smile, catching him off guard. Then I give his junk a swift, and no doubt painful headbutt.

"TIMBER!" I shout out as he falls hard to the ground in a painfilled heap. "Don't touch any girl's body without her permission!" I growl over to him as I get back up and walk over to the other women huddling together.

In the meantime the other Bears come running over to see what's happening. "What the fuck?" Nemo says, looking down at the fallen man and then back over to me as I sit back down.

"He had it coming!" Comes from a dark figure I hadn't seen leaning on a tree, as the male steps out I see that it's Anton. "He was trying to test the merchandise. Our rules are clear, no sampling."

He was watching the whole thing, I just know it.

"Were you just going to sit there and watch?" I snap at him, feeling super annoyed.

With a smirk in our direction, he turns back around and walks away. The nerve of these guys!

Nemo steps forward, helping up the Bear-man. "Fuck dude.

What were you thinking? Go to bed, I'll be on duty tonight, it's much quieter than the day shift at least." He throws a quick scowl in my direction, and I smile back unapologetically.

The guys all disappear except for Nemo and we slowly get comfortable again. "Are you okay, Alice?" I enquire softly.

"Yeah, I'll be okay. Just a bit sore, I might have a bruise in the morning." She sniffles out, trying to be tough.

I sigh. "I'm so sorry that you got hurt but thank you for helping me. Without your help, who knows what would've happened."

I hear Havana whimper and Alice says, "I would do it again in a heartbeat. We have to help each other if we're going to get out of this."

"I couldn't agree more. Night girls, let's get some rest so we have energy for tomorrow." And we all try to do just that.

THE NEXT DAY was a lot like the one before, luckily, in the morning, after we all had a bathroom break, my hands got tied up in the front again. Mostly because Anton figured out that he would have to feed me and give me water, and I laughed about being waited on. It's brilliant, and I can't help smiling at the small victory.

Thankfully it's a good time of year to be trudging through the woods, not too hot during the day and not overly cold at night, we at least had that going for us.

After stopping again in the late afternoon, we're given an early dinner again, the brother Bears and a darker Bear-man that had been staying far away from us the whole time, tied all of us girls around the trunk of a large tree. Each of our wrists were tied to the person next to us. Which is going to suck if I get an itchy nose.

I sit here and listen as I hear the guys discussing the next kidnapping. One of the brothers says, "We'll go this time, Anton, you stay here with Nemo and we'll take the other two. It shouldn't be an issue, the girls are secure and we're far enough out that you shouldn't come across anyone while we're gone."

"I agree." Anton replies, "It should go off easy enough with the four of you, we'll be fine here."

The darker guy puts in gruffly, "If they give you any cheek just knock 'em out."

"Happily." Nemo looks directly at me with a smirk.

Then they go into detail about their plan, they don't seem to know exactly who's at this next location, just that there are four girls and they'll just grab who they can among them, as long as they don't leave empty handed.

I feel really nervous about this, I don't want any other girls to be stuck in the same circumstance as us, it's bad enough that we're here.

"Aren't we enough?" I call out to them. "There's no need to get more girls in on this."

Nemo laughs darkly, "The more girls we take, the more money we make. Stupid pet!"

Darn it. It's so awful not being able to do anything.

The Bear-men head off, leaving us with Anton and Nemo and a sick feeling rising in my stomach.

"It's alright ladies, we'll be fine. It'll be over before you know it, I just bet that there are a bunch of people that see this theft going down and follow them back to us. You'll see, no need to fret." I speak up cheerily.

"Will you shut up for once! Nobody's going to help you. You're just a commodity, get that through your thick skull." Anton snaps at me.

I shake my head. "You're wrong, we have friends and family here now, people will be looking for us."

Anton scoffs, "Them maybe, not you. You're the most annoying female ever made, I'm sure of it, you don't know when to close your mouth, you have no respect for your betters, you're obviously not very smart, and your only useful trait is that you can reproduce. Face it, pet, all you're good for in this world, is to lay on your back and procreate."

My mouth drops open in shock. "W-Wh-What would you know? You don't know me. People like me, people love me here." I stammer and look down and away in discomfort.

He walks over and squats in front of me. "Nobody loves you here, pet! They just love that you have a pussy and a womb. One day somebody will love that mouth, but only when it's stuffed with dick." He shoves some fabric into my mouth to prevent a reply. My eyes well with tears. My biggest fear growing up was that someone would only want me to bear their children and keep my mouth shut. Here, this man is telling me that's exactly what my life on Rathe will be. Barefoot, pregnant, and unequal. I feel a tear streak down my cheek as he stares down at me with something close to disgust. How can someone that makes me shudder with lust one day, make me feel so insignificant and small the next?

Anton's eyes watch the tears trail down my face before he leans forward and licks one off my cheek. "Souvenir." He smirks at me. Getting up, Anton turns around and walks away, leaving me feeling totally irrelevant for the first time in my life.

"Don't listen to him, Janice." I hear Havana say after he walks away in her quiet, husky voice, "I love you. So do Bell and Summer, never forget that."

"Listen to your girl, Janice. We just met you but you've tried so hard to make this bad situation better, with laughter and stories. I appreciate you and your mouth. He's just a bully trying to tear you down, don't let him." Nateesha's kind voice says, and Alice agrees with a small sound.

I squeeze the two hands next to my own in appreciation because I can't talk with my mouth full. I'm so grateful for the friends that I've made on this crazy journey. What a wonderful bunch of women to surround myself with in hard times.

CHAPTER FOUR

We fall asleep like that after a while, tied against the tree and vulnerable to the elements.

However I wake up to scuffling sounds, mens raised voices, and the whimpering of a female. It's dark and I can't see much, only the outline of bodies from the light of the moon.

"Hold her, she's wiggling too much." I hear in the darkness. "Take her over to the others."

People approach, and I can hear them around the back of the tree where Alice is. "What's going on? Let me go." I hear a new girl cry in panic.

"Move over, pet. Sit down! Now!"

I try to wiggle free as I feel the rope slacken around me, it's getting looser but not quite enough.

"Fuck! They're coming! Someone found us. Get the girls, quick." One of the Bear-men starts shouting.

I try to scream as loud as I can with a mouth full of fabric. The girls get my idea and start screaming, *"Help! We're here!"*

"Shut the fuck up!" I hear someone get smacked, the skin on skin contact reverberating in the darkness.

Then all hell breaks loose. Wolves come flying past me, and some other animals. I can't see what type but I hear a cat of some sort and maybe a Bear or two. The wind around me blowing with the movement and the scent of the earth scuffing filling my nose and making me sneeze.

There's yelling and screaming, a gurgling sound to my left followed by a roar and the smell of copper that I just know is blood. The girls behind me are screaming and I use my hand to pull on theirs, I pull them up to the rope trying to signal that we need to get it looser, they understand and we all start struggling to get free.

"I'll help you, I'm still free. Keep still." I hear from the new girl.

"Thank you. Thank you so much." Alice cries and then comes around in between Nateesha and myself, I make a mumbling sound and she reaches over and takes the fabric from my mouth, leaving my tongue and lips dry.

I try to lick my parched, cracked lips. "Thanks." I croak and clear my throat.

Just as our rope drops, a man comes running over to us, it's the Bear-man that tried to touch me. He grabs Alice's blond hair while the other girl comes around to help untie Nateesha's hand from mine.

When we're separated I yell, "Help Alice! I'll undo Havana and me. Go!" The girls take off toward the Bear-man holding Alice.

A Wolf comes out of nowhere and grabs hold of the Bear-man's arm and he lets Alice go with a cry. The girls grab her and turn back to us. "No! Go, girls. Go!" I scream, wanting them to get the heck out of here.

The Wolf is followed by two more, as they bring the, now Polar Bear, down. It's bloody and gruesome, seriously hard to watch. His limbs are ripped and torn from his huge body, the once white coat is now covered in dark splotches of blood as the full moon shines on the scene from above.

The girls turn to run and a Cheetah turns into a very naked man in front of them. "Come with me, I'll take you to safety, we have to run." The girls look back at me and Havana pulling at our ties.

"Run!" Havana cries out, in the loudest voice I've ever heard her use and so they do. They run to safety together. Thank goodness.

I get our binds undone just as Havana's grabbed suddenly and ripped from my grasp. She squeals loudly as she's torn away from me. "Havana!" I yell. I get up but I can't see properly as they disappeared into the dark thicket of trees and I don't know where they went. "Havana!" My voice reaches out into the darkness, desperate for her to call back.

I can't hear her, not one muffled sound, I can only hear the sounds of battle and pain that surrounds me as the Bears fight off our saviours.

I turn and run into the woods behind me and hope for the best. I run for maybe five minutes before... *Smack!* I faceplant against something giant and fluffy before falling back on my butt.

"Ouch!" I say as I hit the ground, rubbing my aching nose. I look up and see a big Grizzly Bear standing in front of me, towering over my fallen body and I mean he's a big son of a gun. Holy moly, I'm done for. Then the Bear shifts into a man and I find myself staring directly at an impressive penis. It may be dark but I'm not blind.

I stare at it and stutter, "Ah, sorry."

He squats in front of me so that his face is up close to mine and

I see that he's not one of my kidnappers, I also happen to notice that he's fine as all heck.

"Are you okay? I'm not here to hurt you." The mystery man says to me with concern in his voice and his hands raised in a show of safety.

I'm still kind of shocked. "Naked. You're naked." Is all that comes out of my mouth.

He chuckles and it's the sweetest sound, so genuine and melodic. "That I am. Let's get you up and you can jump onto my back. It's best if we get as far away from here as possible until the criminals are dealt with." He has a big handsome smile as he says it. "I'm going to shift into a Bear again honey bee, and I want you to climb on top of me, you're going to ride me."

"Yes, please." I feel myself flush because I was all for riding him but maybe before he shifts.

He leans in closer to me and inhales deeply before visibly shuddering. "Mmmm, honey bee, is right. You ready?" I nod dumbly at his pulse inducing words, swallowing hard and unable to speak for a moment.

He gets up and helps me to my feet, I notice before he turns around that he's even more impressive now that he's clearly hard. Apparently I'm not the only one feeling a bit turned on right now.

He shifts into a big Bear and then gets down as low as he can. I'm glad that I'm strong and flexible because he's still really big, even like that. Lifting my leg over, I climb up onto his back and wrap my hands around his shoulders. Then he takes off and I have no choice but to grab big tuffs of his fur to stop from slipping off and I wrap my legs tightly around his big girth. My mind slips into the gutter at that thought.

He runs fast and hard, I slip back and forward on his back, my core rubbing up against him the whole time heating up my insides even more. Holy moly this feels both really taboo and really good.

I start getting tired after about an hour and can feel myself slipping down every now and then, he must feel it too because not long after that he comes to a stop, lowering himself back down to the ground for me. I slide my body down his and land tiredly back on my feet.

Turning back into a man, he steps forward cautiously grabbing my shoulders. "You're tired, honey bee." It's a statement, not a question.

"What's your name?" I softly ask as I yawn.

Smiling he replies, "Keneth, but my friends now call me Chuckles thanks to a new acquaintance of mine."

I laugh lightly, "I've heard of you. Summer's one of my best friends. She's told me all about you, I'm Janice. So, Chuckles stuck, did it?"

"Sure did. Any friend of Summer is a friend of mine." Keneth holds out his hand for me to take. "Come on now, let's get you some sleep."

I take it and he keeps a hold of it as we go to the hollow of a tree. "This should do nicely, it'll keep you out of the elements. Do you mind being the little spoon? I don't know if you can pull off a big spoon." Amusement laces his jovial tone.

He's not wrong. While I'm a long legged five-foot-eight, this guy's a big blond God of a man. Maybe six-foot-two if I had to guess and chiseled with muscle too. Wowza.

"Wait, what?" I just realised that he said he was going to spoon me. "You're naked. You can't spoon me!" I cross my arms with a huff.

He chuckles at me again. "Don't worry, I'd never touch your body more than that, without consent. I'm an honourable and worthy male." He places his hand on his heart to emphasize his point.

"Are you trying to sell yourself to me? That kind of felt like a sales pitch." I enquire, squinting my eyes in suspicion.

"No. I was being honest, but you don't have any males yet, do you? Would I be able to try to win you? Honourably, of course." With an undeniably cheeky tone of voice.

"Lets just sleep for now, buddy, and go from there. No funny business, Chuckles." He laughs at me with such a happy sound that I can't help but smile and warm to him. I fully understand why Summer called him Chuckles, he's clearly a happy, nice guy, I could definitely do worse.

I get on my knees and crawl under the tree with Keneth right behind me. "May I spoon you, female?" I'm grateful that he's not assuming and asks my permission.

"Yes. Go on then, I'm so tired that I really don't care, but I'm trusting you." I say through another yawn.

After laying down behind me, Keneth scoots closer and wraps one big, strong arm around me, placing the other arm under my head like a pillow, and leans his chest against my back but that's the only contact he's made with his body and I appreciate him trying to make me feel comfortable by reducing contact with his lower parts.

I fall asleep in moments, feeling unreasonably safe under the circumstances but I can't help feeling like this man's here to protect me, not hurt me, and I trust that feeling. I trust him, I decide.

CHAPTER FIVE

Mmm, smells so good that my mouth waters. Like maple trees, cinnamon and berries. I snuggle in closer, breathing it in with a sigh.

I feel warmth rub between my legs and I hold close to me the hard, yet silky pillow. I feel my hips involuntarily rock back and forth, slowly grinding myself into this delicious smelling thing. A man, it's got to be a man. I smooth my hands over him and feel nipples stiffen under my caress, and hear a deep moan of longing. Oh yes, I want him. I nuzzle my nose in, smelling his sweet cologne, it's so good, so strong. My hands smooth down rippling muscles, lower and lower until I feel the head of a moist penis and I take it into my hands. Stroking, pulling, smoothing up and down.

The groans get deeper, his breathing becomes panting and then a big hand grabs mine and holds it still. Why? I want him, I'm so wet that I can feel the moisture building at my core.

"Stop. Please." A shaky, deep and desperate sounding voice pleads with me. Hmmm, wait... Is this a dream or am I awake? I snap my eyes open to see a very naked man still in my grip, looking at me with longing.

Darn! What am I doing? I'm draped all over this man, Keneth. I was molesting him and rubbing myself on him. How humiliating.

I sit up suddenly, yanking my hand back as if I was burned. "Son of a gun, I'm so sorry!"

I shuffle myself back feeling absolutely mortified by what I'd been doing to this poor man. Tears spring to my eyes and heat flushes my face, I'm such a bad person.

"Hey, hey." Keneth says with his hands raised in surrender. "I'm so sorry. I didn't mean to let you do that, I thought you were awake. Shit!" He rubs his hands hard up and down his face, looking terribly forlorn.

I shake my head. "This is my fault, I should never have touched you like that without your permission, I'm so awful. Please forgive me, I didn't mean to." I cover my red cheeks with my hands.

Keneth cocks his head to the side, "Wait are you upset because you think I didn't want you to? That doesn't make any sense, I thought you just didn't want to touch me. I'm fine, better than fine. I've never had anyone do that before and it kind of blew my mind. Please touch me whenever you want, you always have permission to touch me." I laugh at his slightly uncomfortable rambling.

"No, I clearly wanted to but I thought I was dreaming. You smell really good." I accidently say at the end. "I mean... I just... you just... I... Um... Yeah."

We both go silent and then look at each other and start laughing hysterically at how silly we're being.

"Just to be clear, I really liked that." Keneth says after calming down, smiling wide at me, his penis still very much hard I notice when I look down at it. "Sorry, that's going to take time." He tries to cover it with his hands. "You're the most beautiful female I've ever seen and you were just rubbing my dick and grinding your sweet pussy onto me. I don't think it's going away anytime soon."

I feel another flush of heat as my vagina clenches from his honest words, I smile coyly at him and shift a little bit to ease the aching I'm feeling.

I see Keneth sniff the air before a growl escapes his throat. "I love honey." Rumbles from him, as his eyes bore into mine.

"Why do shifters do that? Smell the air like that?" I ask, between my too heavy breathing.

"Our sense of smell is very high and it can tell us what an individual's scent is and how another person is feeling by how they smell." He says to me slowly and smoothly. His voice sends tingles down my spine.

I feel my chest heaving even more, "How do I smell?"

He groans deeply and leans toward me, so close that I can feel his breath on my skin. Closing his eyes, he smells deep in the air before snapping his eyes open and staring into mine. "Your scent is like honey and the sun, but right now I can smell that your sex is very wet and aching. The honey smells so strong that it makes my mouth salivate for a taste of it, nothing in this world has ever smelled so sweet." He slowly licks his lips.

I rub my thighs together and involuntarily moan. I whisper back, "You smell like cinnamon, fresh berries and maple trees to me, I really like it. Is that your scent?"

Moving his mouth to mine, not so that we're kissing but just enough to feel the softness of his lips while he speaks, he says, "Yes honey bee, you can scent me, I think we're kindred. I'm so drawn to you, I feel like I need you more than I need to breathe. Will you let me kiss you?" His breath is my breath, he feels so right. I lean in that tiny bit and lick his lower lip before gently taking it between my teeth.

In the next second I'm in his arms and he's kissing me so

deeply, with a fervour that I've never experienced before. His lips are so soft, his tongue is gentle and yet passionate in my mouth, our mouths are devouring each other in the sweetest bliss.

I lean back and pull him down with me, I've never been shy about sex, I've had quite a few boyfriends and friends with benefits over the years but I'd never wanted any of them as much as I wanted this man on top of me.

His blond hair falls around his eyes like a cocoon as we indulge in our lust, I open my legs and he lays between them, my skirt lifting to my hips as we rub against each other. Then I remember that I've got no underwear on, I feel his smooth hardness rub along my centre, through my dripping wet lips.

"Oh, fuck." He groans into my mouth as his strong member gets saturated with my juices. "You're so wet for me. Your body wants me inside you, it wants to take me into your pussy, I can feel it. Tell me yes and I will." He continues to rub against me, tormenting my clit with his back and forward motion.

He pulls my black shirt up, revealing my lace bra enclosing my small perky breasts. With one tug he rips it open and they pop free, my pointy, rose-coloured nipples are hard and aching.

Leaning down Keneth takes one gently into his mouth, twirling it with his tongue and then tugging it gently between his teeth.

"Yes." I cry, "Please, I need you inside me."

With his deep groan vibrating my nipple, his hand reaches down between us to dip a finger into my wet folds before circling my thrumming clit. The head of his penis pushes slightly at my entrance in time with his fingers ministrations. Deeper and deeper his head pushes inside me as I roll my hips, feeling the pleasure building inside of me. "Don't stop." I plead so close to coming apart, between the rubbing and the pressure of him entering me at the same time.

With one hard thrust and roll of my clit, I feel my orgasm explode from me, clenching my walls around Keneth's impressive thickness. My walls pulsing and pulsing, he begins to thrust into me again and again, bringing my pleasure to whole new heights as I scream out into the woods unable to stop myself.

Taking my mouth again with a passionate hunger, Keneth rams his dick into me so deep and fast that I see stars. Keneth leans back up and he grabs a hold of my hips, lifting them higher while pounding into me and the change in position rubs my g-spot just the right way and I feel myself building again. Impossible. I never cum this easily but if he keeps this up I will again. "More! Please, more!" I groan out as it intensifies.

"With pleasure," he says, thrusting even harder. Then it hits again, I scream out for a second time, my vagina clamping down on him and he roars, "Mine!" as it pushes him over and he cums deep within me, spurt after spurt. Filling me up as we both yell to the world and to each other. A perfect end and a perfect beginning.

Keneth collapses on top of me shuddering one last time, we breath each other in and try to calm the storm we made. All of a sudden he rolls over, taking me with him and I lay across his front, my head on his chest, my sheath still filled with him.

"I can feel your heart beating." I softly say snuggling into him.

I feel his chuckle radiate through him. "I sure hope so. Are you comfortable, honey bee?"

I smile into his chest, "Yes, very." I look up and into his eyes, "Am I yours now?"

"Do you want to be?"

"Maybe."

"Well then, I'm yours and you can be mine when you're ready."

I crinkle my face, "So you're mine? Why?"

Taking my face into his and leaning forward to kiss me gently,

Keneth says, "Yes, I'm yours from now until forever. Why? Because we're kindred. I know it, and I'll never let you down. I am happy to wait for you to accept me but I'm not going anywhere."

I know he means every word and that's equally beautiful and terrifying.

"Can we sleep some more or do we have to move?" I ask, changing the subject.

He smiles knowingly, tucking stray hair behind my ears sweetly, "Time to carry on, my honey bee, I'll go and check the parameter and then we'll head off. Maybe I can find you somewhere to bathe first."

With that he gets up and gently pulls me off him, laying me softly to the side and starts to walk off, looking back at me with a brilliant smile, "Stay here and stay safe."

Little did I know, he wasn't coming back.

CHAPTER SIX

I straighten my clothes, dust myself off and try to fix my mess of my white blond bird's nest, that used to be hair. Time passes and Keneth is nowhere to be seen.

Just as I start to worry, I see a big Grizzly Bear trodding slowly up to me. It's so weird trying not to freak out about a big Bear but I still get that feeling of dread that's natural to a human when one approaches me.

"Where've you been? It feels like I've been waiting for an hour. Did you get into any trouble?" I ask to try to dampen my fear, needing a response from the creature to reassure me.

The Bear just keeps slowly approaching, I guess I'll just be riding off without talking then.

"Are we going straight away?" I ask nervously, the Bear nods firmly and I feel instantly relieved. Thank goodness, for a second there I thought it was a real, non-shifter bear. "Ok, lean down and I'll hop on, I was hoping to wash up a bit first. Did you find any water holes?" The Bear just shakes his head and lowers down. "Oh well. Hopefully, we'll find one along the way. You destroyed my bra, lucky I don't have big breasts or this trip would be way bouncier." I laugh at my own joke as I climb aboard my Bear.

He takes off straight away and I hold on tight, I'm doing a better job at it today because I'm awake and alert. After what must be half a day's worth of travelling I tap on his shoulders. "I'm hungry, Chuckles, feed me." I say laughing and feeling merry but hungry and tired.

Nodding my beautiful Bear walks a bit faster and around the corner of some big rocks, to find a watering hole. "Wow. That's so pretty. Can we stop for a swim?" My answer is a galloping Bear diving straight into the deep water. Splashing and rising back up to the surface I sputter, "Hey, not funny. My clothes are all wet." I swim to the side and walk out, stripping as I go.

After I'm naked, I hang my shirt and skirt on the rocks to dry and head straight back into the water. I don't care about being naked in front of Keneth, he's mine after all. That's such a weird thought but it was explained to us how this whole Kindred thing works.

"Are you going to stay like a Bear or are you gonna come here and give me some lovin'?" I taunt, floating on my back in the water, bare breasts warming under the heat of the sun.

The Bear comes over to me and I lower myself in, I wade gently over and look at my gorgeous Bear. "You are truly magnificent, you know that? The most beautiful Bear I've ever seen." I say smiling at him and stroking his muzzle with tenderness.

He ducks under the water, diving below me, and then I feel two very human hands gliding up my legs from behind. I close my eyes as they glide slowly all the way up, curving at my ass, caressing me, then I feel soft kisses at the back of my neck and his arms surround me and pull me against his hardness. "Oh so you do want some lovin'?" My eyes still closed, I lean back against his shoulder as he caresses my stomach and breasts.

I feel him shake his head in the nook of my neck, a deep voice rumbling in my ear, "No, sweets, I want to fuck you!"

My eyes snap open and horror fills my stomach. *Oh my gosh, it's Anton!*

I push myself away as hard as I can and he lets me, I swim to the shore and scramble up, tripping on a branch as I go and landing on my hands and knees.

"Is that how you want it?" His dark, mischievous voice rumbles out behind me. I turn quickly, sitting on my butt as Anton slowly rises from the water. Holy heck he's cut. My eyes are wide as I take in his erect and large penis bobbing as he walks. "You like what you see, sweets?"

"I don't understand!" I mutter in shock, shaking my head and looking back at his face.

Standing in front of me with his hand out to help me back up, he replies, "What's there to understand? He's gone and now you have me. Don't worry, we only have a few more days of trekking and then you'll get a new home."

I wack his hand away and get myself to my feet. "What did you do with him?"

"Let's just say that he won't be bothering you again."

"No." I whimper, my knees feel weak and I pull in a deep, shuddering breath of fear.

Looking at me intently Anton asks, "What, don't tell me you got attached to him so quickly? He was easy to find, you know, I just followed the smell of honey all the way to his dick. You put out pretty quickly, do I get some of that treatment?" He smirks cruelly, eyes hard and challenging me.

"He said I was his," I say defeatedly, sadness filling my lungs as I try not to cry.

"There's a good chance he just wanted your pussy wrapped around his cock. You do also realise that you'll probably have more than one Kindred, right? No need to get all emotional."

"How do you know? He might be the only one who wants me. I let him down, I should have gone with him. How could you do this?" I feel terrible, Keneth was such a great man, my man. My vision blurs as unavoidable tears well in my eyes.

Walking towards the water, Anton calls back over his shoulder, "That's enough theatrics now. Come and get back into the water, you've dirtied yourself again. At least you don't smell like him anymore, that was awful."

I look down through my tears and see that I'm covered in dirt, I slowly make my way back down to the water's edge to clean the dirt off myself.

Anton catches two fish and cooks them up for us to eat for lunch but I just sit quietly, feeling melancholy. I know there's no way to outrun him and at least I have the knowledge that the girls aren't here.

"Where are the other girls?" I question while we eat.

Anton shrugs, "I know that three of the girls got taken back but your quiet friend was taken by Nemo. We split up and said we'd meet up at the destination, it was quicker for me to track you and pick you up on my own, the girl would have slowed me down too much."

I scowl at him, "I'm surprised you didn't get here earlier. What took you so long?"

"Did you miss me, sweets?" He winks at me, clearly amused by my misfortune.

I scoff and ignore his stupid question but I feel him looking at me all the way through the meal. "What?" I finally snap, scowling deeply at his outright stare.

With an arrogant half smile he replies, "I like you being naked, it's much nicer than the clothes you wear, especially when you relax and your legs part so that I can see where your honey comes from."

I snap my thighs tightly closed and scowl at him again. "That was rude to say."

"Why? It's the truth." He just shrugs like it's nothing. "I'll do a lot of things, Janice, but I'll never lie to you, you can count on that."

That catches my interest, "If that's true then why are you doing this to me?"

"Watching you?" Anton shrugs. "I told you already, plus it gives me memories that I can pleasure myself with later."

"You are so vulgar!" I snap, my voice disgusted.

"Yeah, maybe, but you like it. Remember I can smell you and when I said that, your honey got even sweeter." Getting up and stretching his body out, his junk on full display, he moves around to sit next to me on my log.

"What are you doing?" My shock evident.

"I figured if you didn't want me looking at your juicy pussy then I should probably move because I had one hell of a view sitting over there." He sniffs the air and gives me a knowing half-smile. I hate that he's right but my body just reacts to everything he's saying like there's a steady thrumming beat at my core that only he knows how to play. Suddenly, he adds, "I need the means to be more powerful, by capturing you or any female for the market, I get paid well and get a spell of my choice performed by a powerful wielder. A man has needs, you know. It's nothing personal."

"What would you ask for?" I'm curious as to what this man classes as worth my freedom.

He looks at me blankly, "That's not your concern, pet." Standing up Anton continues, "It's time to go now, we have a big trek ahead of us because we've got to go the long way now and I want to get back to it. Go and get your clothes, then get back on top of me." He stops and puts his thumb and forefinger to his chin, like he's thinking hard. "Unless you want to ride me another way, I know I'm not meant to sample you but to be fair you've already been sampled."

I turn and walk off towards my clothes in a huff, glancing back I see Anton checking out my ass with a look of need on his face. I think he would like sex from me, if I gave him a chance, too bad I won't.

After getting dressed, I hop on the now waiting Grizzly. "I'm going to call you Grizzly from now on because you're such a meanie all the time and you growl when you're talking to me."

With a huff from Anton, we take off again to who knows where.

CHAPTER SEVEN

It feels way more awkward than it did the first few times I rode a Bear, mostly because it makes me uncomfortable knowing that my crotch is on Anton's back.

When night time falls and we continue the gruelling task of trudging through the wilderness, I nudge Anton hard saying, "Stop already, I'm done, my thighs and arms are burning from holding on."

All I get in return is a grumpy huff and no sign of stopping. I let go and slide down his back landing on the ground with a thud. *Ouch, my butt.* That wasn't my smoothest move but I'm sore and I'm tired of being carried around like a bag. I'm as keen as the next person for a hike through the woods but I'd rather do it walking.

Anton turns and looks into my eyes with those deep, dark, scary pools. I have to hand it to him, he's one scary Bear when he wants to be. Thank goodness he's not allowed to eat me.

On all fours, Anton gets right up in my face and growls low. Okay, now I might pee myself. "Calm down, Anton, you're scaring me." He growls even deeper, his breath huffing on my cheeks, sending goosebumps all over my body and I have to fight my instinct to run as fast as I can.

I squeak involuntarily as his lips lift, showing me his terrifying teeth, I take a slow step back as my body quakes with fear, my palms grow sweaty and I can feel my heart going a million miles a minute. "Nice, Grizzly." I step back again, voice trembling, "You're not going to eat me are you?"

Taking another step back my heel gets caught in a rock and I tumble onto my butt again, my hands falling back to catch me and then a twig pierces through my palm. I cry out in pain, squeezing my eyes shut.

When I open my eyes I watch as the Bear slowly morphs into Anton on his hands and knees crawling on top of me, in between my legs. "You're bleeding." He murmurs as he moves over me. "Give me your hand."

I slowly lift it up to him and he sits up in between my thighs, taking my hand into his. Anton pulls the twig out and blood drips down my forearm. "It's not too bad, you should be more careful." Then he grabs the sleeve of my shirt and rips it off with one tug, wrapping my hand with the fabric from my sleeve, he ties it together. "Why were you so scared when you know I'm taking you, unharmed, to the market?" He asks me suddenly, his gaze boring into mine.

"You looked so scary and I thought you might want to eat me," I say shakily, my palm thumping with my heart beat.

"Mmm," he groans, leaning back over me so that I have to lay down onto my back. "I do."

Pulling my shirt up slightly so my navel is exposed, he dips down and smells my stomach before trailing his tongue around my belly button. I moan softly as I feel my core clench, I don't know why he affects my body so strongly, I don't like him and yet he makes my vagina throb with need whenever he's close to me.

"I have a feeling that when I eat you, you won't mind it one bit." His hands grip my knees, spreading them further apart as he rubs his nose along the seam of my skirt from hip to hip, my pelvis tips forward slightly. "You have the sweetest, most delectable scent, it makes my mouth water to taste you and eat up all your honey." Anton slowly brings his hands down from my knees travelling up my thighs, taking my skirt with him, so slowly that I can't stand it. I want him to stop and I want him to touch me. I need to make a good choice but I also need his tongue on me.

My head's spinning and I can feel my core starting to drip between my folds. A slight breeze caresses my most vulnerable area and I shiver. I hear Anton growl deeply as he pulls my skirt right to my hips, exposing me fully to his view and I can feel his thumbs stroking where my thighs meet my body. So close, yet so far.

"Look how wet you are for me, sweets. You have the most beautiful pussy, it's better than I ever imagined it would be. It's glistening, pink and dripping with honey." He lowers himself running his nose up my thigh, scenting me. "Tell me you want me to taste you, tell me to lick you clean and I will. With pleasure."

I can feel his warm breath on my wet lips as he gets closer and closer, and feel his rumbling voice on my trembling thighs. I can't think, I just need it. The whole world seems to smell like leather and wood, a manly scent wafting from this sexy, scary man between my thighs, tempting me with his very touch, the very air he breathes.

My pussy clenches again and again, desperate to feel him on me, devouring me. I moan as he blows on my core, my hips leaning up in response, my need growing and getting out of control.

"Tell me, sweets. I can scent how much you need me, how much you want to cum on my tongue as I eat you all up, one lick, suck, and nibble at a time." Anton's voice is an impossibly deep rumble.

I look down at him and see him staring up at me with lust and hunger burning in his eyes, "Tell me, I won't touch you until you do." He runs his tongue along his bottom lip and I follow it, wishing it was on me.

"Taste me." I barely get out between my panting breaths, but he hears me.

A wicked smile forms on his full lips before he replies, "My pleasure." Slowly, while his eyes are still locked on mine, he lowers himself, all the while his thumbs stroke closer until they're almost on my folds.

I can't look away as I watch his tongue slide out, he moves his hands aside to lick up the seam of my leg and pussy, making no contact with where I need him the most, then he does the same to the other side. So carefully, Anton places his tongue on my left fold, licking it from the bottom to the top, repeating the same thing on my right. Never touching my slit or my nub, that's desperate for his attention.

"Please," I cry, moving my hips, trying to make contact. I see Anton's eyes twinkling with victory before he lowers himself down to where my cream is leaking and laps it up with a groan. Then he opens my lips with his thumbs and gently touches his tongue to my clit making me simultaneously moan and shiver at the contact before diving his tongue into my slit, licking and sucking as I rock my hips on his face.

Moving back up to my clit, he circles it gently over and over again before lowering back down to thrust his long tongue into my pussy, fucking it with his mouth.

"Yes," I cry out as my hands go to his soft bald head and gyrating my hips for more, I cry out again as he sucks on my clit hard, alternating from sucking, to licking, to tongue fucking me. The combination is so intense that it makes me shake with need.

As I get closer to my incoming orgasm, Anton pushes one big finger into my tight sheath before adding another and curling them up onto my g-spot. "Shit, I'm gonna cum." I moan out, needing my release so badly, I've never felt anything so good as Anton's tongue and fingers.

"That's it, sweets, cum for me." He growls while continuing to finger me. He latches back on to my swollen clit, sucking and nipping it, sending me barreling over the edge. My orgasm hits me so hard that I see stars, throw my head back in ecstasy, and scream his name.

Anton gently strokes all over my swollen, still throbbing pussy as he tastes me, cleaning me of all of my juices as I come down from my high, pulsing against his soft touches.

I catch my breath as he rises back up my body, nipping at my taught nipple through my shirt as he does, making my back arch. "I told you I wanted to eat you." Anton says smugly, "That wasn't so scary was it?"

Then I come to my senses and realise what I've just let him do to me. "Well that was unexpected," I reply, knowing I should feel bad about it but there's no way I can regret an orgasm that good. I freaking saw stars, for crying out loud.

Anton suddenly jumps to his feet and puts one hand out for me, "Now that your honey is taken care of, let's get moving, we have places to be and people to see."

Darn it. "You're still going to take me to the market, even after that?" I ask, shocked.

"As good as your honey is, and it's fucking delicious by the way, I still have a job to do." He starts walking away, "Move it!"

I twist my lips in disapproval, "Fine, but I'm walking, I'm not riding on your hairy ass anymore."

He laughs but continues forward on foot and I try and fail to not look at his sexy as all heck behind, as I follow along.

CHAPTER EIGHT

We walk in relative silence for another hour before coming across a cave next to a water hole with a small trickle of water running into it.

Anton walks toward the cave with purpose. "We stop here for the night. It's going to rain soon, I can feel it, and the cave will keep us out of the elements for now. I'll start a fire under that ledge on the side for now and then hunt so that you can eat, it's been a long day and you'll need sustenance. See if you can gather anything soft you might want to lay on for a bed, there's no point in trying to escape because I can smell you and I'm much faster." Anton explains as we head under the lip of the rocks above us.

"Fine. I'm not an idiot, plus I'm starving, see if you can bag us something big." I look over at the water and the trickle pouring into it from above. "Is that good to drink?"

Nodding Anton turns to leave. "Help yourself, it's a fresh water hole."

"Great, I might clean myself up a bit before it gets too dark to see." He just shifts and trudges back into the woods where we came from.

I manage to find some grass and leaves and make a makeshift bed. It's not great but it should keep the chill off my bones from the stone floor while I sleep. Heading over to the watering hole, I take off my now very dirty, ripped, and smelly shirt and skirt and hang it off a tree branch nearby to air out because there's no point washing it if it's about to rain, I would hate to be stuck wet and cold tonight.

I slowly walk into the water and under the fresh trickle of clean water that falls down when I'm about knee-deep in and drink as much as I can from it, I'm feeling parched from going most of the day with no hydration. After I've had my fill, I wade deeper into the water until I'm neck deep and rub my body clean while submerged, it's very clear water and I have no illusion that my body's not hidden in its depths. At this point, I think it's pretty moot to cover myself after this afternoon's intimate situation with Anton, which I'm still shocked that I let happen.

Anton comes through the thicket of trees with four rabbits. While not taking his eyes off my bobbing head in the water, he walks to our temporary accommodation, places them down and strides straight back and into the water hole with me, not stopping until he's face to face with me, his breath on my cheek.

We wade there together for a moment, being in the present and looking into the eyes of each other before I say, "Good hunting?" to break the spell we're under.

Humming his agreement, Anton reaches out and puts some of my hair behind my ear. "I was dirty." I randomly say because this silence is weird and yet not totally uncomfortable.

Raising one eyebrow at me with a sly smirk Anton rumbles, "Yes, I imagine you are."

I can't help but smile and give out a soft laugh, "Not like that, you cheeky thing, and you know it."

Anton's usually dark eyes glitter with humour, "Are you sure about that? I distinctly remember you screaming my name while your thighs tried to suffocate me not very long ago."

With that, I squeal and jump on him, attacking his ribs with tickles and lordy this man bursts into laughter. Apparently, Anton's very ticklish indeed. Who knew?

Of course, that just spurs me on further and I tickle him more furiously as he twists and turns trying to escape my torture, laughing his deep booming laugh the entire time.

Suddenly he grabs me under my arms, lifts me up into the air, and throws me back into the water away from him as I squeal in delight. My head breaking the surface again I yell, "That's cheating, I had you." Laughing lightly into the air. "Take it like a man." I go swimming back over to him but he grabs my arms, twisting me around so my back is to his front and my arms are held across my chest under my breasts. "No fair," I try dramatically to wiggle free and just end up squished even closer to his body.

Growling deep in my ear after nipping my lobe Anton rumbles, "Keep doing that and you're going to need to get clean all over again." I feel his large erection pressing against my buttocks as he grinds his hips to make his point.

"Oh." My face flushes red and I feel myself heat up.

"Yes, oh is right. Not that I'm complaining," He licks up the side of my neck before nipping my shoulder lightly.

Breathlessly I say, "You can let me go if you want."

"I don't want to." He grinds against me again and I can't help but tilt my hips back, arching my back so that he can slide between my cheeks and I feel myself grow a whole different kind of wet.

Anton growls, "You're playing with fire, sweets, you should never tempt a Bear with a juicy rump."

I giggle softly and turn my face to look at him over my shoulder, "Do you like my rump, Grizzly?" I roll my hips on him, feeling him sliding between my tight globes. I do this a few times, feeling him tense and grind back into me, all the while we stare at each other, breathing heavily.

Moaning softly and parting my lips, he uses the opportunity to dive his mouth on mine hard, his tongue delving along mine, taking all he wants from the kiss in a possessive, almost painful way. Anton lets go of my hands and places one large hand on my hip to encourage our grinding and the other one pinches my right nipple. How can something hurt and yet feel so good at the same time?

Breaking our kiss, Anton turns me in his arms and lifts me up so that my small perky breasts are at his mouth level, I wrap my long legs around his wide chest and he teases my nipples with his tongue, going from one to the other before sucking and nipping at my left one. My head's thrown back on a moan and I grip my hands on his shoulders, nails digging in as he talentedly uses my nipples to drive me crazy. My nipples have always been a direct link to my vagina, they're so sensitive and just this can drive me close to orgasm, if he even touches my clit I'll explode.

I look down at him and his careful worshipping of my breasts, I breathe out, "Why?"

Stopping, he looks up at me before sliding my body down his, my aching core rubbing along the bottom of his eight pack all the way down to his cock, making me moan deeply again. "Why what?" His voice is raspy and filled with unsaited need.

"Why are you doing this to me if you're just going to sell me? You don't feel a connection between us?" I pant out, feeling very worked up at this point but I need to know if it's just me that's feeling this. I don't know why but I feel a pull towards him that I can't deny anymore, everything is happening so fast and I know he's technically the villain here, but why doesn't it feel like that?

Anton closes his eyes tightly, places his forehead on mine and then sighs deeply while pushing my body back gently, and I unhook my legs and drop in the water again.

"You can't blame a Bear for trying to get laid, can you? You're very tempting merchandise, but you're merchandise all the same." Swimming back to shore he throws back, "Finish cleaning yourself off, I'll get the food ready."

Wet and frustrated, in more than one way, I stare at his departing back in disbelief. Oh my goodness, it's just me. He thinks of me as a product and nothing more. How naive could I have been to think otherwise? I can't believe I let my hormones get the best of me, just because he gave me an orgasm earlier, that's got to be all it is. I need to remind myself that this isn't a fairytale. Ach, I feel dirty all over again. So I wash once more before getting out and putting on my, admittedly still yucky, clothes.

We eat dinner in silence around the fire before heading deeper in the cave where my makeshift bed of leaves lies, the rain finally showed up and the fire slowly died away telling me it's time to sleep.

I lay down on the leaves and sense that tonight won't be great, I feel so embarrassed about my lapse in judgement earlier and I can't look Anton in the eyes anymore.

It's not often that I feel small but tonight I feel tiny and cold to my core. Not so much because of the weather, even though it's much colder tonight than it has been, but because my usual optimistic view of the world feels lacking right now.

I know I shouldn't dwell on the negatives but I'm sure I'll wake up tomorrow with better countenance, I'm probably just tired. I'm sure that if the 'good guys' found me last time, they'll find me again.

I think about Keneth then and I feel dreadfully sad, my heart heavy with grief for a man I barely knew but he felt so right in my arms and I knew that I was his from the moment I saw him. Anton surely couldn't have killed him, he was too nice to kill, too sweet. Maybe he just lied to me and Keneth is out there somewhere waiting to see me again. I have to hope that's true because I can't even entertain the idea of never seeing him again. It's weird because I only knew him for one day but I feel like that day changed my life. This whole kindred thing is crazy.

"Sleep, female." Anton grumbles in the dark, "I can hear your mind ticking from over here, we have a lot of ground to cover tomorrow to reach the next stop before nightfall."

I sigh, roll over and start my fight for sleep. It takes me a while but I get there eventually.

CHAPTER NINE

Another two days pass us by in slight discomfort after my humiliating assumptions, we travel by foot and by Bear, and only once come upon another person... if you can call him that.

Walking in the mid afternoon sun, Anton stops suddenly and looks up with obvious tension running through his body, his shoulders tighten, his hands fist, and his face turns hard.

Grabbing me and pulling me behind his back he snaps harshly, "Stay close and don't move."

I hear a loud whooshing and feel the air around us move before the most beautiful looking man drops to the ground in front of us soundlessly, with giant pristine, fluffy looking, white feathered wings stretched out wide. They almost glow in the rays of the sun and I have to shield my eyes for a minute with Antons body before it dulls down enough to check, and when I look again his impressive wings are now folded neatly behind him, long enough that they're almost touching the ground.

I've never seen such beauty in my life, tears prick behind my eyes as I look upon his flawless, soft skin and perfectly sculpted face. His own eyes, a brilliant gold that glistens in the sun like they have a life of their own, his full lips curved into a magnetic smile. His body tall, lean, and moulded into a woman's dream, his very complexion a golden glow.

Collapsing to my knees behind Anton, I sigh out, "Wow." My mouth and eyes wide, the shock and awe of his appearance clearly written on my face. A single tear slides down my cheek and I feel like I can't move or breathe, only stare at his magnificence.

This man before me is an Angel, of that I have absolutely no doubt. The purity and power rolling off him is undeniable and I'm breathless in its wake. The Angel looks from Anton to me with a small smirk and a tinge of curiosity in his glittering gaze.

"A human. Marvellous." He speaks, or more appropriately, he chimes melodically. His voice is both seductive and musical all at once. The thought of an angelic voice is correct in so many ways, it's a wonder to behold.

"Close your mouth, Janice, you're drooling," Anton's grumble comes out angrily, he doesn't even look down at me when he speaks because he hasn't taken his eyes off the Angel standing before us, not for a second. It's then that I notice Anton's fighting stance, if I didn't know any better I would have thought that it was to protect me from this iridescent creature in front of me, this holy gift from God. It makes no sense.

The Angel rings out with a glorious laugh at Anton's behaviour, giving me goosebumps all over my body, what a benevolent sound. "Hello, beloved human, come to me."

I slowly rise and go to step around Anton but he snatches my wrist and holds it tight. "She's not going anywhere. What do you want with us?" Anton's jaw clenches tightly as his grip increases until it almost hurts.

The Angel tilts his head to the side, looking at Anton like he's merely a bug on the Angels shoe. "This is your Kindred, Bear?" voice soft but curious.

"No." Anton states with narrowed eyes, "But she's my property until she's sold at market, I won her fair and square. If you want her, you can bid like everyone else. Guardian or not, I have a right to keep her until then."

Smirking at Anton, the Angel inclines his head slightly before looking back at me. "I am Ariel, child, I will not take you this day but I will see you. Come here." Taking his eyes off me, he gives Anton a pointed stare. Clearly warning him to let me go.

Grunting, Anton's tight grip on my wrist ceases and I step slowly towards Ariel, the Angel. I can't help it, I have to go, I have to touch him and I walk right up to him and look up into his golden eyes with wonder. He's easily seven-feet tall, and chiselled as if from stone.

Smiling down at me sweetly, he lifts his hands and softly smoothes the back of his smooth hand down my cheek. "Magnificent!" He breathes down at me, my body shivering at the contact. "You are quite the creation, I believe I shall enjoy having humans in Rathe, it has been a long time coming. Maybe I will get one for myself." His mouth purses in thought, "Hmmm... Quite the temptation."

Stepping back and removing his hand from my cheek, his wings unfurl behind him and I close my eyes respectively to the light that reflects from them. "Thank you, Bear, she is rather lovely. Enjoy your discovery. I may visit one of these markets you speak of." Ariel says matter-of-factly.

I frown in disbelief. "Wait? What? You're not going to admonish him for stealing me and treating me like property?" He snapped me right out of my awe with his careless words.

Turning his head to the side again as if in confusion he asks,

"What did you expect, human? That is why you are here after all, to find an owner and breed like a good girl."

My head snaps back as if I was slapped. "Excuse me?" I step back trying to make space between us, all of a sudden I don't feel so safe in front of him anymore. Majestic he may be, but that doesn't mean he has the best intentions for me.

Ariel shakes his head in disbelief, his long white-blond hair swaying with the movement. "Truly fascinating, I was under the assumption that Raziel had informed you of your duties on Rathe, perhaps he wasn't clear enough at Threshold. Pity." Smiling at me brightly, like he isn't treating me like an irrelevant being, he turns to Anton, "You should help this child to comprehend her purpose here, we don't want to have any misunderstandings. The sooner the better, Bear."

With that, Ariel flaps his wings and soars back into the sky, the earth and leaves around us fluttering with the gust of air left behind, leaving me feeling shocked and devastated that this beautiful Angel was not the saviour that my soul hummed for.

"Let's keep moving," Anton's voice pronounces suddenly, walking in the direction we were headed before, with not an ounce of remorse over what just happened.

"No. Are you serious?" I cry out at him, my arms flying up and an edge of hysteria in my voice. "What's happening here?"

Huffing loudly he stops and turns around, irritation evident in his gruff face. "For Celestial's sake woman, I've already told you. How many times and from how many people do you need to hear it? You're here for procreation! While one faction of mhanu believes human women to be sacred, the other faction thinks of you as pets. Unfortunately for you, I am the latter of the two, I'll sell you at the market for my own gain and you will be bought by someone who wants to breed you like the cattle you are here. The Guardians don't give a shit one way or the other, we're all irrelevant to them, Human and mhanu alike. It's all a big fucking game to them because they're immortal and it's just their job to keep us in line. Do you get it yet?" His hands go out wide to the sides, to show his frustration at my lack of acceptance. "For fucks sake, I had to steal a stupid one." He mumbles while shaking his head at me.

I visibly flinch at that, I've never been known for being smart but I'm kind and that's all that matters in the end but it doesn't mean that it doesn't hurt my feelings when people point it out. "I'm not stupid." I reply, my voice weak and cracking with the emotion that I feel, "I just refuse to believe that with all the rights and equality that we have on Earth as women, that it means nothing here. We fought with blood, sweat and tears to have the same rights as men and now that we have that, in most of the world anyway, we've come here just to find out that we have to fight for them all over again? No!" I fold my arms across my chest, "You'll value me as a woman because I am valuable. I am not a piece of meat!" I stomp my foot like a child but I don't care. This is ridiculous and I won't take it.

"The pack I stayed with treated us like Queens, I thought it was overdone because I really do believe in equality, I'm not better or worse than you. We're the same in value, I don't care what sex or species you are or I am. Your value only declines by your behaviour and attitude towards others, not by who or what you are." I rant, frustrated. I feel really passionate about this, there's nothing worse than men or women believing they're better than the other, it's such a disappointing view to have. While we are all different, we're equal in worth.

Shaking his head at me sadly he just walks away, once again proving his point of how valuable he finds my opinions, "Hurry up or I'll carry you over my shoulder." His voice calls back.

I don't know why I even gave this guy a chance. Sure, I'm

certainly attracted to him and my body reacts whenever he's near, not to mention his desirable smell but I'm smart enough to not let my body decide my actions. Aren't I?

I reluctantly give in and follow Anton, knowing I'm not getting out of this and I'm tired of being lugged around. I really thought for a minute there that Ariel had come to save me, not treat me like an animal at a zoo. Today my faith feels stretched. Why would God make his Angels so heartless?

After catching up to him, I tap him on the shoulder as we walk side by side to get his attention, "Anton?"

"What now, sweets? I've never known anyone to talk as much as you do, and about fucking nothing too. Are you incapable of silence?" He doesn't sound angry though, just resigned to the fact that I'll keep talking.

"Well," I start, "I have some questions." My mind is filled with thoughts that I have to voice and questions that I need answers to.

"Of course you do," he mutters with a heavy sigh.

I can't help but snicker at that, "Whose Raziel? I mean, I know his name as an Angel of God, but I don't remember seeing him at Threshold."

Sighing again Anton replies, "You knew him as Boss I believe. He's always been the keeper of Threshold, since the beginning of us all, I think."

That's interesting to me and totally unexpected. "I had no idea Boss was an Angel, I can't believe the Angels here are so awful. Are there good, kind Angels too?"

"You say that as if Earth's Angels are better. They're the same freaking Angels, they just don't go around pissing you off there. And no, the Angels are all the way Ariel and Raziel are. Righteous pricks, the lot of them. The Valkyries can be even worse, those bitches are brutal as fuck, you don't want to cross paths with one of them if you can help it." Anton explains, scratching his stubbled jaw in thought.

"Do they work together? I thought Valkyries were a myth like Odin and all those false Gods."

He stops suddenly and looks down at me like I'm stupid, "I told you before, there's more than one God. You don't listen very well do you?" He continues walking on, a little faster like he's trying to lose me, but I catch up pretty easily.

"What do you mean by more than one God? How can there be?" I ask, feeling exasperated and not liking the direction of this conversation, at all.

"Think of all of the Gods you've heard of as myth and legend. Where do you think that came from? They're called the Celestials for a reason. There are many Gods, all with a different purpose, different level of power, different followers and different jobs. The Guardians were made by two separate Gods to watch over the experiment that is us, so that not one individual set of God's had the total power over *us*, it works for them because the others are more content with watching than partaking and both of the God's selected have nothing to do with the other due to conflicting ideas. It keeps it semi-fair so to speak." Anton looks down at me while we walk, a slight frown marring his face, it's obvious that he doesn't approve of the system. "You see, these two Gods are the most unlikely of them all to converse or barter with mhanu and Humans, because they have the Guardians do it for them. While the Guardians will work for any Celestial that requires something of them, they have their main Gods as the final say in a situation, their creators.

"Here in Rathe we've always been told the truth, while you're all left with relying on one faith or another that half of the time doesn't make any sense. It blows my mind how easily you're all swayed when it comes to religion, and how little you all question anything. We have been taught about how you humans live. You do realise that religion is man-made, not Celestial made? Don't you?"

I feel upset by this, "No. I don't... How can... What?" I rub my face. "This isn't right. What you're saying is blasphemy, I pray to my Lord and there is only one true God. I have faith and it will not be undermined by you."

Laughing out loud, Anton chortles, "As I said, you're stupid and you don't listen. Don't talk to me if you're going to be ridiculous. We live in fact, you live in fiction. I think it's hilarious that humans think that we're the fictitious species, yet you comfortably choose to live in lies." He rolls his eyes and scoffs loudly.

My eyes fill with tears and they slip down my cheeks silently. I feel like my life is a lie, that everything I have ever known has been based on betrayal. I have never questioned my faith and I don't want to start now.

Looking down at me Anton puts his arm around my shoulder with a quick squeeze, "There's no need to be sad. Your God is very real, sweets, and you have proof of it now, the only difference is that you need to make peace with the fact that he's not alone up there. If you think about it, that should make you happier, not sad." He pats me on the back and then walks ahead of me like he didn't just do something sweet again. Anton's such a conundrum, I don't know how I feel about all this but I know that he doesn't want me sad and that's enough to make me smile despite my tears. There's hope for him yet, and I choose to hold on to that.

CHAPTER TEN

As night falls, Anton pulls us under the hollow of a tree where there's a large burrow of some kind.

"What is this?" I ask as I crawl into the burrow, it's only big enough for us to both lay comfortably next to each other and tall enough for Anton to kneel in. Coming in behind me, Anton sits down just inside the entrance.

"It's one of the burrows I've made over time. I keep them all over so that when I'm too far from home I can sleep safely. By tomorrow afternoon we'll be at my den."

"I thought you were taking me to the market, not your den? Have you decided to keep me safe instead of selling me?" My voice hopeful and the corner of my lips curl into a smile.

Anton looks over at me bleakly, "No, the market's only half a day from my den but I do have a shower, food and a comfortable bed that you can stay in before you head to the market. It's the least I can do, I suppose."

I pull my knees to my chest, hugging them tight, and I place my chin against them, trying to make myself small. Fear, a real thing living inside me. I look over at Anton, "You're better than this, I know you are. What could you possibly wish for that's more important than my freedom?"

"You could end up with someone kind and from the other faction for all you know. They might show up at the market to rescue the females. Did you ever think of that? It might not be so bad." He proposes with a shrug.

"You can tell yourself that if you want to make yourself feel better, but we both know it's more likely that I'll end up as some kind of sex slave that has to kill myself to escape the torture and pain that I can't bear anymore." I cry out, letting my biggest fears have sound. Hearing them out loud makes it so much more real, so much so that my chest seizes in pain and I start to hyperventilate. Deep wrenching sobs get torn from my throat that I just can't contain anymore, giving further life to the terror that I've been trying so hard to fight with optimism and hope. Now the fear flows as freely as my sobs and my body's wracked with it.

An arm goes around my shoulders and pulls me in and I find myself pulled onto Anton's strong lap, his hand smoothing down my back while I sob into his chest untempered.

"Shhhh." He hushes in my ear, trying to calm my raging storm of emotions. "Janice, please." His hand goes around the back of my head and he holds me to his chest tightly for comfort. I stopped caring that he was naked days ago, it's just a natural state to see him like that now, to someone outside this situation we'd probably look odd. A large naked man with a slim clothed blond sobbing uncontrollably in his lap.

"Please, sweets, I can't bear to see you cry like this." I feel him kiss me on the top of my hair and breathe me in but it doesn't stop my torrent from flowing.

I am terrified. All my life my brothers have protected me and I was taught how to protect myself by my Daddy, but now I'm just a prisoner. A product to be bought and sold, there's no one to protect me now and I'm too out of my depth to protect myself any more than I have so far. I never would've imagined being so weak as to sob on the lap of a man that put me in this position in the first place.

Lifting the bottom of my shirt, Anton tries to wipe my face and nose. I'm ugly crying, the kind that no one wants to see, he has a lot to clean. I eventually change from my deep heart wrenching sobs to the slow, sad kind that sounds as pathetic as I feel right now.

"Come on, Janice." Anton whines, "You're making me feel bad." He strokes my hair back from my face gently.

I sniff and look up at him. "For crying out loud, Grizzly, you should feel bad, I'm a person, not cattle." Tears still stream down my cheeks.

He looks down into my sad eyes and I can see real guilt shining back at me. Good. He darn well better feel guilty, he's the one doing this to me, I knew he was nothing but bad news.

With a deep sigh, Anton puts his hand on my cheek, rubbing it back and forth with his rough thumb. "Sweets, if I had another choice then I'd just let you be free but you've got to understand, I've been waiting for an opportunity like this for almost two hundred years, it might not ever happen again for me. I'm sorry."

I squint my eyes in confusion, "Huh?"

"What?"

"Did you say two hundred years? How old are you?" I ask, astonished.

He smiles slightly. "Age is different here, I'm sure you were told within the ten months that you've been here. We age like you do until we hit twenty, then our aging slows right down and by the time we reach a hundred we look about twenty-five and roughly age ten years physically, every century from there. Therefore even though I look about thirty-five to you, I'm just under two hundred."

I sit back and look at him in shock, "Well I'll be! How does getting a human Kindred work then? You just have a partner until she gets old and dies?" My sadness was forgotten for a moment, because I'm now in full curiosity mode.

With a small laugh he answers me. "Once a Kindred coupling is made, their lives become intertwined. In other words, when they die, you die or when you die, they die. Your life will be connected to their longer lifeline and you'll begin to age at the same rate as we do but if one of you is killed, that's the end for both of you. The Kindred left dies almost instantly of a broken heart." Anton explains while still holding my face and looking deeply into my eyes, it feels a little bit intimate but I don't want to break eye contact just yet.

"What happens if you have more than one Kindred? Does everyone die when one of them does?" I question further, in awe of how it all works.

Anton pulls me back into him, placing my head on his chest sweetly and stroking my hair before explaining, "If the female dies, all the male's hearts break but if only one male dies and others are left, the female feels the pain of loss forever for each one that she loses, but lives until the very last Kindred life has been lost." Anton hums while still stroking my hair unconsciously, "It's both really sweet and really sad. For any child between them, they lose both of their parents at once and that can be very traumatising. Unfortunately it's not an uncommon outcome here." I feel like he's speaking from experience because I can hear the pain in his voice and his tender actions are showing me that he needs his own comfort as well right now. Is the loss of his parents why he's the way he is?

We sit like that for a while, with me on his lap and him stroking my hair. My sadness has mostly passed and I sit here and contemplate the kind of existence that would entail the depth of love for someone that would break a heart so deeply that it stopped forever.

"How do you make a Kindred coupling official so that you're joined for life?" I ask after what feels like an hour of comfortable silence.

"Sex with a Kindred spirit, it's how we claim what's ours. Once you've been claimed or have claimed someone, you can't take it back, it's for life." Anton's voice sounds somewhat absent, like he's just as deep in thought as me.

I purse my lips and turn to look at him, my face probably much too close to his. "Keneth was my kindred, we both felt it and he said so himself, we made love right before he disappeared. Does that mean my life is linked to his now?"

Anton frowns, "He said that, did he? Are you sure that was a true statement and not just him trying to get sex from you? It would explain why you smell so different."

I nod confidently, I know what I felt.

"Then yes, you'll live while he does."

"So you didn't kill him then?" I smile, feeling a well of relief. "Or I'd be dead too."

Shrugging noncommittally he replies, "Guess I didn't hit him as hard as I thought I did. Good thing, huh?"

I scowl at him, "Ah, yeah, that's a good thing. Will he come and find me?"

Anton shifts uncomfortably under me, looking out the burrow hole. "Should do. He must be pretty badly hurt to have not caught up to us by now though, he might still be knocked out and could die yet realistically. Otherwise, I imagine he would've found us already." He looks at me with eyes wide, realising at the same time as I do that maybe things might be worse than we originally thought.

I gulp hard, "Oh." I feel myself pale at that. "That's not great news." I try to move off Anton's lap feeling suddenly very sick, my stomach roiling and threatening to bring back my dinner. He holds me still by my hips and turns me around, moving my legs over to straddle him.

Grabbing my chin with his thumb and forefinger he lifts my gaze to his, the look of regret deep on his face, eyes sad and his mouth downturned. "I'm sorry, I knew you'd slept with him but I didn't really believe he was your Kindred until now. You are positive, right?"

A silent tear escapes down my cheek, "Yes, I'm sure." A feeling of dread in my chest.

"I'm so sorry, sweets." Putting his arms around me in a huge embrace, he pulls me right up against him, tucking my head under the nook of his neck with a sorrow filled sigh. "I never wanted you to die. Please believe that."

I sniff sadly with my ear against his chest, listening to the steady beating of his heart. "What was the wish that you waited two hundred years for? I think you at least owe me an explanation, a reason for taking my freedom and potentially my life. Don't you think?"

I feel his head lean down on top of mine, "I was going to wish that one of the Bear cubs yet to be born would one day turn out to be my Kindred. My parents died when I was very young and I've lived a very hard life on my own for a very long time. I was abused a lot as a child by some awful males. They did things to me that I can't ever erase from my mind and it's all I ever dream of. Through all of that, the only thing that got me through the darkest days of my life, was that one day I wouldn't be alone anymore, that I would find a Bear to be my Kindred and have a family of my own, cubs that I could protect the way there was no one to protect me. It keeps me alive, it keeps me fighting.

"I dream of a world where the only thing I'd have to fight for again is the ones I love, the ones that love me. I want her to be strong and I want her to have other Kindreds too, they'll help to keep her and the cubs safe in case something happens to me, I know she would live and my cubs would always be loved." He squeezes me tight, his voice soft and filled with whimsy. "I truly am sorry, I'd never have asked for a Kindred of my own if it meant killing yours, killing you. I'm clearly not worthy of a Bear of my own, I'm not worthy of a Kindred. How could I have dreamt of keeping a family of my own safe, if I throw the life of others so carelessly away?"

"Don't say that." I feel so sad for Anton, I understand why he did this. His life must have been so dreadful and I can't even begin to comprehend the tragedy that was his childhood, while this life may almost be over for me, it isn't for him. "Anton," I lean back and look up at his sad face, "I'm not dead yet, you can get me to the market on time, I know you can."

"What?" His voice comes out shocked and his eyes search mine, confused.

I smile sweetly at him, "If I can do one good thing with my life then let it be this, take me to the market as soon as you can. I might make it there in time for you to claim your wish, if you can make it before I die, then you'll get your Bear. We can make this work if Keneth's life just lasts a little bit longer."

Anton's jaw drops, "Are you serious? Why are you saying this? Don't you hate me? I don't understand."

I lean up, hold his cheeks in my hands and kiss his lips tenderly, "Everyone deserves love and happiness, Anton, and if you ask me you're way overdue. You're a good guy underneath your bad choices, you'll find peace in this, I can feel it. Promise me that you'll treat her how I deserved to be treated, that you'll be the father you've always wanted to be, and that after your wish is made, you never make another wrong turn like this again. I'll happily give my life for yours, if you can promise me that."

CHAPTER ELEVEN

Watching the single tear flow down this hard man's cheek, I know that I'm doing the right thing.

"Should we leave now? We can walk through the night and be there much faster, it's important that we don't waste time." I try to move off him again but his hands hold my hips in place. "Anton. We have no time to squander."

"You can't really mean this." His voice breaks slightly, as his masculine scent wafts over me, causing me to take a deep involuntary breath.

"Oh, bless your heart. This is my life and I get to make this choice, now chop chop. It's time to move." Still, his hands don't let me budge an inch as I try to push myself free of his unyielding grasp.

Anton rumbles in his throat, swallowing hard and making his Adam's apple bob with the motion, "Female you're driving me crazy, stop all of your wiggling, you're making my dick hard."

I look down, and lo and behold his little bear is standing to full attention, and I'm all of a sudden very aware that I'm commando and straddling him. Looking up I can't help but giggle at his heated expression. "Whoops." I smile a toothy grin, feigning innocence.

All of a sudden, his hand is behind my head and he pulls me in close for a feverish kiss. His teeth nip at my bottom lip, and as I sigh at the contact his tongue delves into my mouth, taking possession of it in a way that only he can. A moan escapes me because I'd somehow forgotten how good he tastes and how hot his kisses made me.

With one hand, Anton moves it under me and grabs my butt cheek, squeezing it and dragging my body closer into him. Pulling my hair hard with his other hand, my head rolls back with the pressure and he nibbles his way deftly along my jaw, before licking up my neck. "You taste so damn good."

Taking my mouth again, we kiss passionately. I can feel his big member pulsing against my stomach and I reach down to wrap my hand around it, hearing him groan inside my mouth as I do.

While his dick is extremely hard, the skin surrounding it is velvety smooth as I stroke him up and down, never ceasing our feverish kiss. His hips buck forward, thrusting into my hand as I handle him and it makes me wet seeing how needy he is under me. I feel so powerful, holding this strong Bear-man in my grasp, while he pulses and writhes at my very touch. "Does that feel good?" I ask seductively between kisses, hearing the heat in my own voice. I stroke him harder and faster, watching how he reacts to me, what he likes and what he doesn't.

"Fuucckkkk!" He grinds out as I nibble on his ear while stroking him just the way he wants me to. "I can feel your juices dripping on my leg, sweets."

Anton's hand goes between my thighs, where my pussy rubs itself on his leg, and he slides his fingers up and down my core, through the wet mess I'm making on his lap. "So fucking wet." His finger slips inside me and my head lolls back as I moan out loud.

"If I'm cuming, then you're going to cum too." He growls as he fingers me softly.

Another digit enters my soaking wet sheath and Anton starts to finger fuck me harder. His palm does torturous things to my clit, making me grind and moan on him as I pump his dick with my tight fist. I bite my lip hard as he watches me with hooded eyes, both of us getting closer and closer to climax together. Without taking his fingers out of me, Anton manoeuvres me to lay on my back with him leaning over me, both of us panting, his other hand pulls my skirt right up to my chest during the move. With my pussy on full display as he works me over, wet sounds filling the cavern, Anton watches himself fingering me closely as I bring him to the edge.

"Fuck, Janice! Cum for me first." He moans out trying not to spill his load before I reach my climax and his heated words push me further. My legs begin to shake, my toes start curling as his palm rubs my nub and his fingers curl inside me, driving me wild.

"I'm gonna cum. Oh, I'm cumming!" I cry out as my core spasms around his fingers, hips bucking furiously as I ride it out.

He takes his own dick in his hands and aims it at my still pulsing pussy before cumming all over it. His hot spurts hit my clit and folds as he growls, "Ohhhh, sweets!"

Anton puts his fingers on my tender, wet pussy and gently rubs his cum all over my sensitive lips and clit, it feels so good.

"I'm gonna make you cum again using my cream to rub you, my sweets." Anton continues rubbing his cum on, in and around me, making me squirm and moan. With these kinds of movements it won't take me much to cum again. This is so freaking hot.

"That's it. You like that, don't you?" He whispers as he nibbles on my earlobe and I moan deeply, my hips gyrating again, feeling my next climax soaring closer, even faster than before. "Oh, fuck." I cry out. One of his moist fingers works down to my puckered backdoor and pushes gently on it, rubbing the entrance while the other hand massages my clit and fingers my pussy. "Don't stop, please." I beg and just as his finger inserts my puckered hole I scream out my second release.

My orgasm hits me hard, I literally scream, climaxing around his cum covered fingers, I tremble badly all over, my back arching off the ground. *Oh my gosh!* His lips find mine and he kisses me deeply, with a passion that takes my breath away. His breath becomes my breath and I hold on to him for dear life, pulling him down on top of me. He rolls over so that I'm half on top of his chest, and we stay like that and kiss for a while, with our combined scents musky in the air, my leg over his hip, and my core pressed against his side, covering him in both of our juices, but neither of us cares.

Slowly he pulls back and looks deep into my eyes and I ask him nervously, "Anton, will you hold me tonight? Please? I don't want to be alone."

"Yeah, sweets. I'll stay as close as you want until we get there. Sound alright?" He replies, sweeter than I've heard his voice before.

I nuzzle my face into his neck, my arms wrapped around his chest, and his arm pulls me in close. "Thank you," I whisper just before I drift off to sleep.

LIGHT SNORING WAKES ME UP, and I look around to see rays of light peeking through the burrow's entrance. Carefully I remove myself from Anton's warm embrace without waking him because everyone knows not to wake a sleeping bear after all.

I crawl out of the burrow and stand up fixing my clothes, there has to be somewhere around here that I can wash my dirty self,

Anton always picks a place near freshwater to rest. I close my eyes and listen carefully around me for any sign of water, I hear birds chirping playfully in the distance and the trees rustling in the light breeze, and finally, the sound of tinkling water not far off to my left. I follow the soft sound and before too long, I come across a small stream not even ankle-deep. I take my clothes off and carefully wash myself the best that I can, squatting over the cool water.

"Well that's a sight that I don't see every day." I jump up in shock and turn around to see Anton leaning against a tree with a smug look on his face.

"Oh my goodness. You scared me so bad, you're gonna be the death of me." My hands angrily on my hips as his smile quickly evaporates and I realise what I just said. "Too soon?" I'm trying to add some humour to a humourless situation.

Growling he stalks over and leans down to kiss my mouth roughly. "Yes. Always." He says, his lips still skimming my own. Then he stalks to the stream and washes his own body while I lean on that very same tree and perve at him for a change.

He looks at me watching and I give him a wink and wiggle my eyebrows. "Well that's a sight I don't see every day." I mimic in a deep voice.

Anton charges me playfully and I squeal and run away, trying to dodge him in the trees before he catches me effortlessly and tosses me over his shoulder, my naked butt right up in the air.

"Cheeky female." Anton laughs and then slaps me hard, right on my left butt cheek, making me squeak. He walks me over to my clothes, slides me down the front of his, hard in every way, body and huskily says, "You better get dressed before I make another mess." His smile is large and suggestive.

"Alright, alright. We should get going anyway to try and get as close as we can, time is of the essence." With that statement his smile slides right back off his face. That isn't my intention but I'm an honest kind of girl and I don't shy away from my responsibilities.

I get myself dressed and ready, as quick as can be and we head off for the next stop; Anton's home, or den as he calls it.

CHAPTER TWELVE

We spend the day talking about each other's lives, while walking to our next destination, holding hands. It's a beautiful day, the sun is shining, the breeze is fresh and soft on my face, and I think to myself that today is not a bad last day.

It's not that I want to die because I never have. I've always loved life, every moment of it, but I can't feel bad about something that I have no control over and Keneth may be fit as a fiddle for all I know and just doesn't know how to find me. If that's the case, then I'll deal with the market the best I can and try to get the word out that I'm there. I'm sure he'll save me, he's my Kindred after all.

It's about mid-afternoon if I had to guess, and Anton's just told me that we're only around the corner from his den. We've made really good time and I'd be happy for a rest, my poor legs have had one heck of a workout this past week.

Anton stops walking suddenly and sniffs the air. His whole body tenses up and he squeezes my hand too tight. "We need to go faster. Can you run, Janice?" His tone is stilted and tense.

Apprehension fills me, "Yes, and I'm pretty fast too if I need to be."

He looks around before giving me his hard gaze, "Good. Run!" Suddenly he lets go of my hand and he bolts in the direction we were headed in and I hoof it as fast as my legs can take me to try to keep up with him. If this Grizzly Bear of a man's scared enough to run like heck away from something, then I know I don't stand a chance with whatever we're running from and I pound my legs as hard as I can, my fight or flight spirit kicking in with full force.

My heart pounds in my chest as Anton yells out, "Faster! Run, Janice, run!" Holy moly, now I'm terrified, eyes wide with fear and arms pumping hard as I go, my legs burning from the exertion I'm putting them through and I don't care. I'm running my butt off and I have no inclination at all about looking behind me. No way.

"Almost there Sw..." Anton is cut off when a giant Grizzly comes barreling out of the trees to his side and tackles him to the ground with a hard *CRACK*.

I ground to a halt in shock, almost tripping over my own feet. Anton swiftly turns into another Grizzly and the two of them start rolling around, looking like they're trying to kill each other. I can't look away but I know it's not safe around two Grizzlies fighting,

I start edging around the area they're brawling in carefully, and just as I get to the other side of them, a heavy breeze blows through and I screw up my nose in complete disgust. *Ew...* I can smell hot, rotten eggs and it's gross. *What is that?* I look back in the direction that we came from and see off in the distance, what looks like a stampede of... I don't even know. Creatures. Scary nightmare-like creatures.

They look about waist high, have long dog-like faces, with lengthy, curved menacing teeth but with jaws that are snapping open and closed so wide that they look like they could swallow a huge chunk of my leg, their tongues lolling long and wet out of the side of their elongated jaws. Their eyes are pitch black and huge, they're running mostly on all four of their long skeletal legs, sprinting towards us so fast I can't fathom it and I notice that their front legs have long clawed hand-like paws at the end. I've never even dreamed of anything remotely as scary as what I'm seeing.

I scream. I scream loud! My eyes wide and my body shaking so hard that I can't move, all I can do is scream as they race towards me, saliva dripping from their distended mouths, the sound of their feet digging into the ground sickening me, dulling out the growling of the Bears fighting behind me.

Both Bears stop fighting immediately and look at me, then to the creatures that I'm screaming at. They both jump up and gallop toward me. The closest Bear grabs my shirt with his teeth, dragging me roughly while still running into what I can only assume is the den that was behind me. He drops me unapologetically inside with a thud, the second Bear right behind us.

Turning around they both run back to the entrance, one Grizzly standing up tall and roaring with a boom that echoes through the cave-like entrance of the den, as if to warn them off. The other one starts heaving a giant boulder close to the hole of the entrance, to plug it closed later, I presume. I look around the area as I get back up off my butt, and see that there's a long, dark tunnel behind me, and a wooden chest off to the side. Running over to it, I look inside for a weapon, and only find explosives; TNT sticks and matches. I grab a few out just in case I need them and hold them close to my body, shivering from fear as I do so.

All of a sudden, those creatures begin screeching an awful, hollowed screaming sound and pounce on the Bear roaring at the entrance. I have no idea which Bear is Anton or who the other Bear is, I just know that I don't want them hurt by these petrifying things. The smell of rotten eggs surrounds me so thickly that I feel like I'm choking on it. Sulphur, it's the smell of sulphur. *What the heck!*

Both Bears are now working together at the entrance, trying in vain to bat away the incoming mass of whatever the heck those things are. The biggest Grizzly roars ferociously as a creature bites down hard on his arm, ripping out a large chunk of his flesh as if he was made of butter. Oh my Lord!

"Come inside, close the door." I scream at them. "Please!"

Another pained roar sounds off, as the other Bear shakes off a creature chomping off the top of his leg in one swift bite. Blood is pouring out of their wounds and into their thick fur coats, while more than a few of those nightmares lap it off the ground, grinning and licking, their tongues so long that they're almost the length of my arms. I cringe at the sight, unable to watch.

The two Bears fight to beat them off and run inside the entrance, both pushing the boulder across as fast as they can, a couple of creatures try sliding inside just as they jam it closed. Squealing sounds out as their arms and legs are stuck between the boulder and the wall, and the limbs writhe and wriggle on this side of the boulder creepily.

I can barely see through the dark though but a flare is lit to my left and I see Anton holding it up, his face pale and sweating, his leg a horrific mess. I gasp out loud at the shock of seeing him like that, my hands covering my mouth. "Oh my gosh, Anton."

I go to step towards him and I glance over to see a blond man sprawled out on the floor, just out of reach of the boulder, he's bleeding profusely from his arm and looking up at me with wide, worried eyes. I would know those beautiful blue eyes anywhere. "Keneth!" I cry running to him instead and dropping to my knees in the dirt. "Baby, are you okay? What do I do?" I drop the stuff

I'm carrying and my hands travel aimlessly around his bloody, naked body, fear freezing me from any helpful actions.

He simply smiles up at me, breathing heavily, "Honey bee! I found you." Then he promptly passes out.

His arm's bleeding so badly that it starts to pool around at my knees, sticky and warm, his coppery scent filling the air along with Antons.

Just then, the creatures start to scratch away at the side of the boulder, chunks of the rock falling away, and their limbs reach through the gaps that they're making with their claws, screeching and crying those hollow screams that terrify me. The kinds of sounds that will haunt me in my dreams for the rest of my life.

"Sweets, we have to move away, they're getting through." Anton says behind me, placing a bloody hand on my shoulder. I turn and look at him and see that he's not doing much better than Keneth, I'm surprised he's able to stand at all.

I get up quickly, "Can you help me move him to the back of the cave? He's too heavy for me and I won't leave him here."

He pants heavily, his chest rising and falling in the flares light with the exertion of standing upright, "I don't know if I can, Janice."

"If he dies, then I die, remember. Are you okay with that all of a sudden? You can do this, I know you can, as soon as we're safe you can pass out too but you have to try, for me." I yell at him in desperation, all the while pulling at Keneth's other arm and he doesn't budge one bit.

Anton drops the flare at our feet and pops another one, throwing it down the tunnel behind us. "Fuck it. Let's go!"

Bending down and taking Keneth's arm from me he grabs him in a tight hold and with a deep huff, power-pulls him as fast as he can, all while limping terribly, through the tunnel of the cave, as if he stops or slows down, he'll drop. "Hurry." He cries out as he disappears into the dark.

I grab the stuff and run to the back a bit before I look back toward the boulder, a few scary heads are now poking through, screeching and screaming and I know they'll get through any second now.

Knowing what I have to do, I hold the dynamite in front of me and light those suckers up. There are five of them, I quickly put a couple at the bottom of the door, one on each side of the door and stuff one in a crevice at the top, avoiding snapping mouths and claws as I do, and then turn and run for my life back down the tunnel. I have no idea if I just made our situation better or worse, but trying something is better than trying nothing and getting eaten.

"Run." I shout down the tunnel, I bolt as fast as I can through the darkness, hoping that I don't fall down a hole or something.

BOOM! BOOM! The explosion is fierce.

The whole tunnel seems to shake and I lose my footing, smashing down on the floor in a messy dive. My senses are overpowered, the boom in my ears, the hard impact of the ground, the wave of pressure from the air colliding with me, the rumble and stones falling all over my body, the dirt flying into my mouth, and the breath leaves my lungs in a heavy *whoosh*. Then a weighty silence envelops me, the only sound being the beating of my heart, before I start to cough deeply from the dirt and dust forcing its way into my lungs, the air contaminated with it from the impact.

The only thing I see is darkness as I pry open my eyelids, wiping away the dirt clinging to my eyes and face. I turn my head left and right carefully in case I hurt myself in the fall, I look behind me as I lean on my elbow but there's not even a tiny sliver of light around me. At least that means the entrance is closed, hopefully good enough to keep those things out, I would hate to be stuck in the darkness with one of them. I shudder just thinking about it.

I don't feel any large pain on my body, my knees, stomach, and arms hurt a bit from the landing but otherwise I'm mostly unscathed.

"Anton! Keneth!" I cough out, hoping to hear any sign that they're okay but only silence greets me in return.

CHAPTER THIRTEEN

I slowly rise up to my feet and feel my way roughly along the dry, scratchy floor until I touch the bottom of a wall. Grateful that I found one, once I'm standing I smooth my hand along it slowly, shuffling my feet along.

There's something really frightening about being in a pitch black tunnel, relying solely on your other senses. I walk along carefully like that, for what feels like a long time before the tunnel turns a sudden corner, as I turn with it, a light shines out way down in the distance. Feeling somewhat giddy about the brightness at the end of the tunnel, I speed up my process slightly, still shuffling my feet along so I don't fall but going a lot faster than I was before.

As I get closer to the source, I enter an open room and find that the light's coming from glow worms delicately placed all over the ceiling above me in a beautiful soft haze of colour, there are so many of them that I can make out the shapes around me in the room.

There's a big bed at the back, with drawers to my left, and

another wooden chest to my right. Going over to it, I duck down and swing it open, finding that it's still too dark to see what's inside, but I feel my hands around until I come up with a thick candle and eventually some more matches, because I lost my first set in the blast.

Lighting the candle, the room illuminates much brighter, the fire light flickering and dancing along the walls and the glow worms turning their shine right down. I decide to take the candle back to where I came from and try to find the boys, they have to be back there somewhere. As I move down the tunnel, I see what looks like some kind of light globes on the ceiling. He must have a light sphere here, it would really help if I could find it.

When I turn at the tunnel again, I notice that if I turn right instead there's a bunch of furniture there and I decide to go in there first in case the sphere is in there. It still blows my mind that they have magical spheres that act as electricity to everyone's households. Very handy and very cool.

Just as I enter what's obviously a lounge room, I catch a glimpse of the sphere to my right, moving over to it I turn it on, my hand pressing down into the centre as I was taught when we first moved out of Threshold and into the villages here.

"Let there be light," I say quietly as the entire den brightens, I squint my eyes at the intense change from dark to light and let my gaze slowly adjust.

When the brightness no longer stings my eyesight I look behind me and the tunnel is mostly illuminated but I still choose to take my candle, just in case. Walking down the other end with ease now that I can see clearly, I pay attention to the fact that the lights do stop at some point in the distance. I knew I'd walked far but I hadn't realised how far until now.

Just as the light appears to die into a sea of darkness, two large bodies lay on the floor unmoving at the precipice, I put my candle down safely and run toward them, they look so bad that I gasp and try to hold in a sob. I must have shuffled right by them without even knowing which is surprising considering the coppery scent of their blood that now fills the stifling air, there's an unhealthy amount of it seeping out from under their combined bodies, morphing together in a morbid display in the dirt.

Anton and Keneth are so closely contorted that I'm not sure where most of the blood's coming from, I just know there's a lot of it and neither of them look good right now, their pallor waning more before my eyes.

I lower myself to them carefully, my already filthy knees resting beside their bodies, Anton's face is the closest to where I am and Keneth is behind him and under his arm. I remove Anton's arm tenderly from Keneth's face and try to wake them, nudging them both carefully, and lightly slapping their faces.

"Anton," I slap his cheeks with no response, leaning over him, I try the same again with the other male. "Keneth, baby!" There's no use, they don't budge at all. I am, however, desperately relieved that they're both alive, their chests heave as they breathe in and out.

I very carefully unravel them from each other and nudge them over onto their backs so that they're side by side and not laying on one another. By the time I'm done, I have a thick sheen of sweat layering my dirty body, and I'm panting and huffing breathlessly because of how heavy they are, and how much energy that took to do. *Holy moly, they're big boys.*

After a quick rest leaning against the smooth wall, I go back down to the den and find the kitchen. I get a bowl, soap, and water, and then find a sponge and towel before heading back up to clean the guys off a bit so I can see how bad they are and what I can do about their injuries.

With patience and a lot of care, I sponge bath them both one at a time, making sure to change the water whenever it gets too dirty to help keep them clean. I can only do their fronts because they're way too heavy to roll again but I do the best I can under the circumstance.

After I finish wiping them down from top to bottom, I wash their willies too because I'm a sweetheart like that and I've seen them both before, so it's not a big deal. Finishing off, I dry them thoroughly and take time to inspect their wounds properly, at least the ones I can see. I have a feeling that Anton has a big one on his back because new blood keeps seeping out from underneath him.

Next, I go searching for some kind of first aid kit, while I'm definitely not a nurse, I have to try something. I search the den and start to think that I'm never going to find one, and just when I think about ripping up Anton's clothes, I found the kit underneath his bed. *Score!*

Bending over Keneth first, I carefully try to wrap his extremely mangled arm, a literal chunk of his arm is missing and I can easily recognize his bone in the middle of the bloody mess. *My gosh, what were those things?* Thank goodness I don't have a weak stomach.

Keneth's arm comes across as the only bad damage he's obtained, so I move over to put a dressing on Anton's equally messed up leg.

"Sun of a gun, boys, you've gone and made a mess out of yourselves for sure." I breathe out quietly as I work on securing the bandage once I'm done. "Lord have mercy, you're both lucky to be alive."

"Mhmm." Keneth agrees as he turns his head slowly with a grimace and looks at me.

"Keneth, darlin'." I almost shout, jumping back over to his side, relief flooding my bones. "Oh, Chuckles, I never thought I'd see you again. You came for me! You're alive! I was so scared that you were dying somewhere." I gush, kissing him all over his face gently in-between my words of affection.

He chuckles weakly under his breath, "Honey bee, of course I came." He moans then, and whines in pain, his good hand grasping at his mangled arm.

"I'm sorry, I can't move you, I tried but all I could do was lay you flat and clean you up a little. I haven't found any medicine to help with the pain but I wrapped your arm. I don't know what else to do honestly." I cringe at his pain, feeling helpless. "Tell me what to do!"

"I have... to rest... a while..." he huffs out in deep exhales, looking like he's going to pass out again, "Go... sleep honey... bee, okay." With no more energy to spare, he rolls back and he passes out once more.

I look between the two Bears before me, wishing I could move them into the bed but knowing I can't. I decide to bring them a blanket and I get up to go search for a spare, finding a decent size one resting on the back of a couch. It'll get blood on it for sure but it'll help keep them both warm tonight.

Going back through the den, I take in where everything is, and I find some jerky in the kitchen and gobble it down before heading to what I find to be a bathroom. There's a natural shower-like spray coming down from the grey stone roof, into a hot spring at the back of the room. It's about the size of a small pool and looks just big enough to swim around in.

I strip myself down out of my disgusting clothes that I'll never, ever wear again and I walk myself into the spring, I head straight to the spray and wash my hair under the water pouring from the hole in the roof, a moan instantly escapes my worn body as the heated liquid caresses me all over like a warm hug.

Finally, I'm relaxed, dropping myself into the depths, I lay in the spring floating on my back and for a minute I almost fall asleep. Jolting upright suddenly, I decide that I'd better get out in case I do and end up drowning.

Happy to be clean, I dry myself off on a fluffy towel hanging on a hook, making sure to hang it back up where I found it. Walking through the den naked, I go into Anton's room and rummage in his drawers, I pull out one of his huge t-shirts and slip it on. I'm not a short girl but I'm a petite one so it drapes over me with ease, making the length cover just under my behind and it's super comfortable and soft.

Checking on the guys again, I know I need to rest because I am exhausted after everything that's happened, not just today but this whole week, but I'm so scared that the creatures will get through or that one of the guys will need me during the night. With more than a little trouble, I drag Anton's big, heavy arm chair all the way up to where they're laying, I grab the blanket from his bed when I'm done, and curl up in comfort on the chair by their sides before sleep easily drags me away, to a long night filled with nightmares about dog-like creatures with big mouths.

CHAPTER FOURTEEN

The sound of my own screaming wakes me up. Sweat beaded on my lip, my palms wet with the stress of my nightmares, my body trembling, and I look around confused and lost for a moment, not remembering where I am or why I'm here.

"Honey bee." I hear rasping in the night. I look down and see two men laying on the ground. Keneth, and Anton. Right! My memory comes back to me and I involuntarily shudder.

Keneth creaks out, "You okay?" his voice sounds so pained, his breathing laboured.

I slide down to him, "My love, I'm okay. You're awake. Do you need anything?"

"Water." His eyes are still closed and his words are quiet and raspy.

"I'll get you water, just stay awake." I jump up quickly, running through the tunnel to the kitchen, before coming back as fast as I can with a cup of water. "Drink," I say, joining him again and helping to hold his head up for him.

He sputters and coughs at first but manages to drink a little bit.

I lay his head back down, wiping his filthy hair lovingly away from his face. "Do you need a pillow, my darling?"

Shaking his head slightly he smiles slowly and with great effort replies, "Just sleep... stay with me."

"I won't ever leave you again," I promise as his head slowly falls to the side and is instantly back asleep.

My poor Bears. Keneth never even opened his eyes, and Anton still hasn't moved at all, not even a twitch. My fear for his back injuries grows exponentially by the hour.

Feeling a lot more refreshed now that I've had some sleep, I try to roll Anton enough to see how bad his back actually is. I put his leg and arm over to the opposite side and use all of my might to roll him over. With a great heave and quite a lot of effort, I manage to get him into a relatively good position, considering.

"Oh, good Lord," I mumble as I take in the deep seeping gashes lining his back; dirt, grime, and blood coating the wounds, shocking me. "Anton!" I gasp. His wounds need dressing immediately, I can't leave him like this, I wish I'd been able to move him earlier but I was just too drained. Fear and guilt fills me at the thought of him getting an infection in this desolate place.

Leaving him laying on his side, I rush back to the kitchen to get the same limited supplies I used yesterday and take them over to work on his back straight away. Unable to wrap anything around his torso because of his large size, I use tape to secure the dressing, also washing down and drying the stone floor beneath him, just in case he rolls onto it later. For now though, I'm going to keep him on his side to encourage the wound to stay as clean and dry as I'm able.

I have no idea what the time is or how long I slept for, because I can't see outside and time feels sort of irrelevant here. I haven't found any windows or anything but I'm not suffocating, so there must be airflow coming from somewhere. Deciding to get some more sleep after hydrating myself, I snack on some more of the jerky and cuddle back into my chair, knowing that I need to keep my strength up, since these two are clearly out of the game.

After waking up again from another terrifying nightmare, I've had enough sleep, there's only so many dreams like that I can handle. Checking on the guys and seeing no new response or change from them, I decide to scrub the place from top to bottom, unable to sit still in my rising panic any longer than I have. I have no idea what's going to happen next and the terror residing inside me about their welfare is almost too much to bear and I desperately need to keep busy.

When I finish distracting myself with cleaning the entire den on my own, I dig into Anton's bookcase, looking for something, anything to read. Just as I bend over searching for the right book, I hear a low growl coming from behind me, I jolt suddenly and spin around in fear. My thoughts flicker to those terrifying creatures closing in on me.

"It's just me, honey bee," Keneth says while leaning heavily on the wall, his hand over his bandaged arm. I'm so shocked to see him that I just stand there with my mouth open and my hand to my throat, I can feel my heart pounding in my chest from a mixture of fear and relief.

He smiles slowly, "What, no kiss?"

Striding to him with renewed energy, I stop just before my body touches him. "I don't want to hurt you." My voice sounds so small and quiet.

"How could you possibly think that you'd hurt me, after you just saved my life?" Keneth leans down and puts his forehead to mine, his light blond hair falling around the sides of his face.

My chin rises, and I get onto my tiptoes to give him a soft, sweet peck on his beautiful lips. "My darling," I sigh with my lips on his, my eyes filling with joyful tears, and my chest tight with emotion.

"My honey bee," he replies before taking my lips again in a deeper kiss that feels more like a promise.

I snuggle into his chest on his good side and hold him like that for a while, sighing so deeply that I know a weight has lifted from me. Too soon, I realise how tired he must feel, putting my arm around his waist I start to direct him. "Oh, I'm sorry, let me help you to the couch."

"Actually, is there somewhere I can shower and maybe relieve myself? Those are kind of my main concerns at the moment," he says with a chuckle, "I can't imagine that I smell great".

I giggle back at him, knowing he must be feeling a lot better if he's joking already and direct him to the bathing area. "I'll wait outside while you do your business, call me when you're done so I can help you into the bath. Will you be alright on your own?" Keneth nods with a smile.

I take him to the toilet and use that moment to go and check on Anton and see if he's any better. Finding him lying on his back now but otherwise still unresponsive, I tuck the blanket carefully around him, making sure he's warm before going back to help Keneth in the bathroom.

Walking in the room, I catch him already knee-deep in the water, "Wait for me, I don't want you to slip." I take my shirt off swiftly and hang it with the towel so it doesn't get wet, turning to see Keneth's eyes burning hot as he takes in my naked body from top to bottom.

"Don't look at me like that Mr! You were just mauled by some weird nightmare creatures that I never, ever, ever want to see again by the way." I go to him, hop right under his good arm and gently guide his body deeper into the water until I'm chest-deep. It's just enough that he can keep his bad arm out of the water, because at this rate it's definitely too mangled to get wet right now.

Getting the shampoo, I set to work washing his hair then body, making sure that he's clean as a whistle from top to bottom as he moans and grunts all the while, with only his wound left to go, but I'm going to wash that separately afterwards.

"I feel so lucky to have you taking such good care of me. What did I do to deserve you?" Keneth kisses my cheek lightly.

Kissing him back on his gorgeous, soft lips, I smile up at him, "For one thing, you followed me deep into the woods trying to save me from being sold at a market. I think that's worth me washing your hair, don't you?"

Chuckling at me, Keneth reaches down to cup my behind in his large hand, dragging me against him. My naked body flush against his own, feeling his growing erection between us. My lips part in surprise, but my body responds immediatly, clenching my sex.

I breathe out, "Why Keneth, what kind of girl do you take me for? Do you really think I'm going to take advantage of my injured Bear?"

Closing his eyes, a rumble erupts from his chest, "Call me yours again! There's nothing in all of Rathe, better than being called yours."

My hands pull his face closer to mine, and he opens his eyes as I say sweetly, "My darling, you *are* mine. My kindred, my love, and now my life." I kiss his nose, "And I'm yours, you silly Bear."

"I never knew it would feel this right," Keneth says with a huge smile on his movie-star face, eyes beaming with devotion and joy, "I heard that it was amazing to love and to be loved, but that doesn't quite cut it. There are no words to describe this feeling, you really are a part of me now."

I sigh, shaking my head in disbelief of his perfect features and adoring words, "You're so pretty."

Chuckling sweetly, my Bear replies in a fake, booming voice jutting his chin out, "I think you mean ruggedly handsome. A truly magnificent male specimen." Laughing out loud at the joker that is my Kindred, I slap his chest lightly before making my way out of the bath, holding my hand out for him to come with me.

"Come on, you magnificent male specimen, let's get you warm and dry. There's a bed here with your name on it, you can rest while I get you some food and water."

Helping him to the room and into the bed was not so easy, he started losing his energy fast after that and was relying on me more than I liked. Once Keneth was tucked up in bed, I brought him jerky and water, placing it next to the bed for when he woke up again. He passed out straight after he lay down, the blood loss must have been extreme for him to be so listless.

I put on Anton's borrowed shirt and took up my place next to him in the armchair. I'm less worried about Keneth now since he's been up and is in a bed, but my worry for Anton keeps getting worse. I've had to wipe the sweat off him a few times now and I fear that he's got an infection.

Technically, I know that he's the bad guy in all of this but I've felt a connection with him since we first met, plus we've bonded over this crazy journey, even if we hadn't meant to, especially after we both believed that I'd die.

I truly recognise that there's a very good man under all his poor choices, I can even understand why he felt that he had to make the choices that he did. To be brought up surrounded by so much fear, hate, and pain must have been unbearable for an innocent child, I can only imagine how that could make someone feel cornered enough in their life to be like this. It makes me so sad, and I refuse to be just another person who gave up on him and left him for dead.

One way or another I'll help Grizzly get well again and find a way to make his wish come true. He deserves a happy ending, we all do.

CHAPTER FIFTEEN

A tapping on my shoulder stirs me and I hear Keneth say, "Honey bee, why are you sitting here? He doesn't need your care, and he doesn't deserve it. Come to bed with me."

I shake my head groggily with a yawn after being woken before I was ready. "I don't like him laying on the floor up here where it's cold. He could get worse and die, the least I can do is stay with him in case he needs me." I place my hand on Keneth's, that's now resting on my shoulder, as I look down to Anton's body, sprawled out on the ground. My heart aching at the sad sight of what was once a formidable male.

"But why? I don't understand." He squeezes my shoulder gently.

"Oh bless your heart. Because, my dear Bear, even though he kidnapped me, he also protected me, took care of me, and he was doing it for his own understandable reason. I don't imagine that he wanted any harm to befall me, not really." I look back up at Keneth. "I'll never forgive myself if I leave his side for too long and something happens to him."

"You're a truly honourable female. If this is important to you, I'll see if I can lift him into this chair. We can push him to the den together and you can rest properly and still watch over him." He looks around the sides of my chair. "It reclines, so it'll be fine for him to rest on."

Getting up and looking at them both I ask, "Are you well enough to lift him though? I don't want you to hurt yourself worse, you're far from healed."

Chuckling he bends down and grabs Anton with his good arm, "You'd be surprised what I can do with my body already." Grinning, he gives me a wink, yanking Anton unceremoniously onto the armchair. I rush to help straighten Anton up, making sure he's in a good position.

"That was a bit rough," I snap and Keneth shrugs at me unapologetically. We work together to slowly push the chair down the tunnel and into the lounge with a view through to the bed in the opposite room.

"Now, will you come and rest?" I notice Keneth looks a bit pale and sweaty, and know that was too much effort for him, but at least they're both close now, making it much easier to keep an eye on them.

Hopping under his arm to help guide him back to the room I reply, "Yes, dear, let's go. You need more rest and so do I."

"Rest, yeah, that's what we'll be doing." He laughs softly.

With an eyebrow arched and a 'don't mess with me' voice I say, "Yes! Rest! Only rest. Don't get any funny ideas, Chuckles."

Carefully placing him into bed, I go to his good side to join him, snuggling in close, my arm over his chest and my leg over his thick thigh, I breathe in his berry and wood scent and sigh in satisfaction.

"Did he ever touch you without your permission?" Keneth suddenly asks as he begins to stroke my hair.

"Not really, no." I answer honestly.

I feel him tense. "What do you mean by 'not really'?" He growls out, his hand now still by my side.

"Well, I didn't ask for him to kidnap me, that was definitely against my permission, but that's not what you're asking is it?" I sit up slightly, lean on my elbow and look down at him.

"No, I suppose not." His gaze, firmly on mine.

Pursing my lips I decided to continue with my honesty, "We've touched each other intimately but it was never against my will. I'm sorry if that upsets you, I haven't had sex with him though if that makes you feel any better. I think he's waiting for his own Kindred and doesn't want to risk getting stuck with me instead."

"You're not a booby-prize, Janice. He would be lucky to have a female as perfect as you," Keneth's face sets with a deep frown. "I hope he didn't make you feel less than worthy, because it's the other way around."

I smile softly at him, "No, not at all. It's just that he wants a Bear of his own. I'm not offended by it, I know my worth."

"Thank you for being honest with me." He pulls me down to snuggle close to him again and says into my hair, "You're everything in the world I could ever have wanted, I would never care if you were Human, Bear, or Moose. As long as you're mine."

"Oh, listen to you, you big marshmallow. I'm glad you like me the way I am, because I'm not about to change and I'm not going anywhere." We lay quietly like that for a while, enjoying each other's embrace, and I relax listening to the sound of his steady breathing and heartbeat.

Just when I think he must be asleep, Keneth asks me quietly, "Do you mean that? Fully? Truly?"

"Mean what, Chuckles?" My mouth turns up in a smile, my eyes still closed.

"That you'll stay with me?" His hand gently strokes down my back as he talks, "Will you come back to my den, with my clan to live? For the rest of our lives? You don't want to leave one day?" His voice sounds uncharacteristically vulnerable and scared that I'll deny him, maybe he believes that it's all too good to be true.

"I'm yours, love, forever." With my arm around him, I squeeze his chest lightly to help my point hit home, reassuring him that I'm here to stay.

Keneth clears his throat, fidgeting a little, and I can tell he wants to ask me something but he's not sure how to.

"Yes, Chuckles? What do you want to know?" I can't help but let a small laugh escape because of his obvious discomfort.

I open my eyes to him shaking his head with another one of his, *let's face it,* adorable chuckles. "You already know me so well, honey bee. I don't want to scare you off but I really want to know early on so that I'm prepared." He shuffles a little bit more before continuing, "Will you want to have my cubs too?"

I laugh out loud then, I can't even help it, I laugh so hard my mouth hurts. I lean over him, giving his mouth a few hard kisses in between my laughs. "Seriously? Why did you think I chose to stay in Rathe, instead of leaving?" My laughter morphs into a bright grin, "I already knew there was a wonderful male here waiting to love me, and I was all in from the moment I knew what the choices were. I could feel that God had a plan for me to live here, and who am I to deny Him?" I squish Keneth's cheeks with my palms and look deep into his eyes, "I wasn't disappointed either, and I expect you to give me many babies or cubs. Do you hear me, Mr Chuckles? As soon as we get home, you better get to work because I'm ready to love not just you, but them too."

I watch as his pupils dilate, with a deep hungry growl rumbling out of him, his good arm pulls me on top, to straddle his hips. "Female you keep talking like that and we'll start right now!" He bucks his hips up to grind his large, very hard, dick against my core to prove his point. I let out an unavoidable whimper at the contact.

Moving his hand from my hip, up and under the large shirt I'm wearing, he gently caresses my breasts. His hard calloused hand is rough against my sensitive, pebbled nipple and I arch my back into his touch, while simultaneously rubbing my bare sex against his velvety hardness, getting rewarded with an even deeper growl.

"Am I hurting you?" I ask him gently, pausing my movement.

Grinding me against him again he says, "The only thing that's hurting right now is my full balls, aching to empty inside you."

"You're too hurt my darling, I should get off." I'm so worried about injuring him further, common sense ignoring my vagina's protest.

Dropping his hand down to my throbbing sex as I rise to get off him, Keneth slides his thumb under me, into my tight hole gathering my honey, as he calls it, and then rubbing it purposefully around and on my nub making me moan and stay exactly where I am. "I'll get you off alright but don't you dare move, take your shirt off so I can see all of you."

Against my better judgement, I do. Pulling the shirt over my head, while continuing to rock over the length of his shaft in time with the movement of his torturous thumb, a soft moan escaping my parted lips.

With hooded eyes, Keneth hisses when I reveal my body to him once more, with awe and lust in his voice he says, "I'll never get sick of seeing you like this, you're so perfect."

"So are you, I can't believe I'm so lucky." I pant out, my pussy clenching for more, the pad of his thumb driving me crazy.

"I want you to cum for me, honey bee, then I want you to slip that tight pussy down my hard dick and ride me. Do you think you can do that? You'll have to do most of the work though." Keneth's voice comes out husky and filled with need.

I moan and grind faster on him as he picks up speed, my wetness now coating his shaft and thumb. "Yes." I cry out, getting closer.

Keneth watches me closely with hooded eyes as I rock against him shamelessly, my body on full display, and it's all too much, I climax hard, crying out his name. His hand moves to lift my ass up, and he grinds out, "Ride me, honey bee, I need to be inside you, now!"

Still convulsing I place his engorged head at my entrance and slowly start dropping down onto him.

"Oh my gosh." I moan. Keneth, unable to stand my slow descent, thrusts his hips up hard, filling me to his hilt. The mixture of pain and pleasure, shockingly gives me another orgasm instantly and I scream with my head flung back. He thrusts up again and again with his hips, as my pussy clenches around him. Coming to my senses I take control, lifting myself up and down, riding him slowly at first before increasing the tempo until I am quite literally fucking him.

"Fuck! Yes!" Keneth yells out holding my hip hard, slamming me down onto him with loud slapping noises filling the room. "Cum for me one more time, honey."

I feel so close and I ride my big Bear hard and fast, his cock deeply filling me. When I'm almost there, he reaches down and flicks my clit, spiralling me over the edge. Keneth follows me straight away, with my pussy milking him for every drop as we climax together.

Shaking, my wrecked body slowly flops down on top of his huge body. I take care not to go near his injured arm.

I tremble on top of him and I rasp out, "Are you okay? I didn't hurt you, did I?"

"You were amazing. You *are* amazing." Kissing me on the top of my head, he whispers, "Sleep my honey bee, I love you."

I close my eyes and yawn deeply, suddenly feeling exhausted. With his penis still inside me and my head on his heart, I drift off to sleep. My first sleep with no nightmares since we entered this cave.

CHAPTER SIXTEEN

Groan! Growl! Strange sounds wake me from slumber.

Opening my eyes, I focus on the noise, it's not coming from the room. Turning to look at Keneth beside me, finding him still fast asleep, I realise it must be Anton.

Getting up carefully so that I don't wake Keneth, I put on my shirt and pad out of the room quietly to check on how Anton's doing. I find him tossing and turning on the recliner, in obvious pain.

"Hey, hey." I rub my hand up and down his arm softly, "It's alright, Anton, I'm right here, we're in your den. Can you hear me?" I grab a cloth next to him and start to wipe his face, neck and head. He's sweating so much, I wish I was able to get him into the shower, he really needs it.

All of a sudden, his hand shoots up and grabs my wrist so tight that I squeal in pain.

"Janice!" I hear from the room behind me and before I can do anything, Keneth is there, ripping Anton's hand off me and growling down at him.

I try to push him back away unsuccessfully, "Stop." I say to him, "He didn't mean it. Look at him, he's a mess. Can you get me some fresh water, please?"

Grunting and looking unhappy with the situation, Keneth does as I ask, watching Anton carefully the whole time.

Leaning down closer to Anton I speak calmly, "I'm here for you and I'm going to help you get all better again, you'll see.

His eyelids flicker a little bit, before slowly opening and looking up at me, "Sweets?" He coughs and breathes unsteadily before adding, "What's happening? My leg."

"Hey stranger, it's alright we're safe, those insidious monsters almost ate you up like a big old snack but you're alright now, I've got you, Grizzly." Smiling at him I take his hand into mine.

Keneth clears his throat in obvious discomfort before striding over to put down the fresh water and a clean cloth, "Here you go, honey bee. Why don't you let me do it? I don't want you too close to this piece of shit." He tries to take my hand out of Anton's but I hold tight.

Growling at Keneth, Anton pulls me back towards him, "Fuck off Bear, this is my den."

"Yeah, well that's my fucking female you've got your hand on, if you don't want to lose it, I suggest you let her go, right... fucking... now!" Both Bear-men start growling, each one of them holding one of my hands.

"Right!" I shout out, pulling both of my hands back from them, "That's enough of that. You hear me? Sit your butt down in the lounge or go back to bed, Keneth!" I point to the couch before turning to look down at Anton with my hands on my hips. "As for you Mr, you had better cut it out. I'm going to look at your wounds now and give them a good cleaning, since you're awake enough to move from side to side. Has anyone got a problem with that?" I look between them with a scowl.

Keneth grumbles under his breath, "As long as he knows you're mine."

"He does, my darling, Anton has made it very clear that only a Bear female will do, so calm down."

I wet the cloth and start washing down Anton's face to clear away any new sweat that's forming. "I'm going to put up the recliner now and I'm going to need you to lean forward as far as you can, alright?" My voice is calm and reassuring.

He just looks up at me as I adjust his chair and wait for him to lean over, "Well, come on then, lean forward big guy."

"You won't die now." He says, instead of moving.

I nod, "That's right. Don't worry though, I'll still help you get your wish, I won't let you down. If we have to, then Keneth can organise to break me out as soon as you get it. Don't look so worried, I'd never let a friend down." Smiling reassuringly, I wipe his forehead.

Frowning he says, "You think of me as your friend, after everything I've put you through?"

"Of course silly. A friend is someone that you can count on when times get tough, someone who won't judge you and we have that. Now lean over!" I push his shoulders forward trying to get him to move. "I don't know how long you're going to be awake for."

Obliging me, he does as he's told and I remove the dressings and gasp.

"How bad is it?" Anton asks.

I slowly and carefully dab along his rapidly healing wounds. "One thing is for sure, you guys heal way faster than humans. Holy moly. It looks so much better already, mind you it's still very bad, so keep taking it easy."

Keneth comes over to take a look before explaining, "It's not easy to kill us, our injuries were particularly heinous or we would've been healed by now, my arm already feels much better and it's closing at a rapid pace. Do humans take a lot longer?"

"There's a pretty good likelihood that either of your injuries would have killed me, if not from the blood loss, then probably from infection. We're very easily killed, trust me. A bump to the head is enough to do the job." I continue cleaning and redressing his wound as I speak.

Looking up, I see Keneth staring at me in horror. "I hope you're kidding? How am I supposed to keep you alive?"

I can't help but laugh at that.

"It's not funny." Anton muffles out, "That's very disturbing." He sits back carefully when I'm done, looking at Keneth with a deep scowl, "You'd better be a good male. How are you going to keep her alive if you can't even stop a random male taking her? That's not good enough, get her more Kindreds as soon as you can."

"You don't get a say about that and neither do I. If she gets more, that'll be between her and the Fates. But fuck me, that's scary." Poor Keneth looks pale.

"I thought that I became stronger and stuff when I got you, darling. Isn't that how it works?" I ask, sure that I heard that my health becomes more similar to my Kindreds.

Looking at each other and then at me, they both nod simultaneously looking relieved. It's actually quite comical to watch.

"Now, to look at your thigh," I start, "I'm going to have to lift the blanket quite high to see it properly. Are you alright with that?"

"Not particularly." I hear Keneth say from behind me but I choose to ignore it.

Anton smirks at him before answering, "Be my guest, sweets.

You can take it all the way off so you can see it the best, you don't want to miss anything."

The growling starts up again at my rear. Getting up I go over to Keneth, grabbing him and pulling him toward the bedroom before I push him in and close the door in his face. "Stay in there till I'm done, I don't need your sour mood right now. I want *my* Chuckles back."

Turning back to Anton, I see him laughing softly. "Oh, shush you. Let's have a look."

In one swift move Anton rips off the blanket, leaving himself totally bare to me, his large semi-hard member in full view and I stare at it in shock as it rises, becoming harder and longer in front of my eyes. My gaze goes to his and I find him staring at my long legs, peeking out from under his shirt.

My core tingles at the heat of his stare and I rub my thighs together to quell the throbbing that's starting to build the longer he looks at me with heat in his eyes.

"Come here." His deep voice rasps out, and I find myself moving forward against my will. Stopping just before him, he reaches out and touches the bottom of his shirt, "I like my shirt on you, keep it." The back of his fingers brush against the top of my thighs, right below my sex.

I shudder under his touch as I feel my desire building, he brushes against me again and I exhale heavily. Leaning forward, Anton inhales my scent and I know that he can smell my arousal, I look down and see his thick, hard cock pulsing.

The door behind me opens and I feel Keneth's heat as he approaches me. I don't move though, I know it's supposed to feel wrong like this but it doesn't, it feels so darn right.

With a husky voice at my ear, Keneth breathes, "I could smell you from in there. No more growling, Janice, I promise, just let me taste your honey, it's irresistible." Placing his hand on my hip, he moves his body closer to mine from behind so I can feel his desire rub against me.

Anton lets go of my shirt, dropping his hand to my knees, and then slowly gliding his fingers back up my legs at the seam, his hand touches the inside of my thighs, torturously slow until he finally meets his fingers with my core, my body trembling under his touch.

Keneth kisses me down my neck and shoulder, as his hand rises around me to lightly mould my breast, squeezing my pebbled nipple through my shirt. I moan, unable to help it.

"Fuck." Anton rasps and I open my legs enough to let his fingers slip between my wet folds. He pushes one of his big digits into me, making me gasp for air as he moves his finger slowly inside me, curling it against my g-spot with precision.

Keneth turns my head to face him, taking my mouth with his, kissing me passionately at the same time that his hand dips to go under my shirt and up to deftly trace my nipple with his fingers. With my body leaning against him and my legs open to Anton, I feel overwhelmed by the sensation of their touch.

Moving my head to look down at Anton I see him taking his finger out of my aching sheath, and placing it into his mouth, sucking off all of my juices with his gaze locked on mine. "You taste so good, sweets, I want to watch you get licked and devoured until you cum. Will you lay down on the table and let me watch him take you?"

Oh my gosh, the thought of him watching me get eaten out makes me even wetter, I turn to look up at Keneth who smiles at me with desire, nodding slightly to let me know he's game.

I walk to the table in front of Anton, and sit on the edge, lifting my shirt above my head, putting it behind me and opening my legs for his viewing pleasure. Both men look at my pussy with a ravenous gaze, desperate to taste me, and I've never felt more powerful in my life. Stepping forward Keneth drops to his knees between my legs, inhaling my honey scent and growling deep in his chest.

"Taste her, Bear, I want to hear her moan and see her flush with pleasure, I love the way her skin pinkens as she gets closer to cuming." Anton grinds out in his baritone voice made for sex.

Turning to look at him, Keneth asks, "You've seen her cum before?"

"Oh yeah, I've tasted her cum before and it's the sweetest taste to touch my tongue."

My breath hitches slightly. Is this going to be a problem?

With his gaze back on mine Keneth smiles and agrees, "Just like honey." He lowers his face down to my core, his hot breath on it making me clench in anticipation, and he lets his tongue gently touch and lick around my folds and nub without making contact, the closeness making me moan.

"Please." I beg, needing him to move just a little bit, to lick me right where I need him, my hips arching and moving to get him closer because he continues the torture, moving to gently suck and nip at my lips, tugging on them and humming. "Oh my, please."

Unable to take anymore, one of my hands grabs his hair and pushes his face into me, needing him to touch where it aches. I feel the vibrations of his chuckle as he takes my nub into his mouth and sucks hard.

"Aaaaahh!" I cry out, my head flopping back and my legs shaking with need, "More!" I demand, grinding into his face, as his tongue forces me closer to climax, the feeling so good that I can't think, I need it. I drop my head and see Anton across from me, gripping his girthy shaft and pleasuring himself while he watches me get devoured.

Making eye contact with me, he tells Keneth, "Put your fingers inside her, she needs it." His voice a low panting, getting closer to cuming right in front of me. "Fuck, sweets. Cum for me!"

Keneth pushes one and then two fingers into me, stroking against my walls perfectly and I come undone yelling, "Yes. Fuck, yes." and I cum hard, watching as Anton releases into his hand, jutting his hips and moaning deeply, never taking his eyes off me.

CHAPTER SEVENTEEN

Standing up in between my legs after licking up all of my cream, Keneth smiles deviously at me, "Are you ready for more, honey bee?"

Without waiting for an answer, he stands up, grabs my hip with his good hand, and turns me around, "Bend over." His voice is a sexy growl as he pushes me down with the palm of his hand in the middle of my shoulder blades. I flatten myself against the table, with my ass up in the air and legs spread slightly open, standing to the side a little so Anton can see me bent over, ass and pussy exposed.

"Holy shit, you look good like that." I hear Antons deep voice rumble from behind us.

Keneth caresses my body tenderly from my neck, down to my ass, lovingly gripping my tight cheek before positioning himself at my centre, angled slightly for Antons viewing pleasure, the head of Keneth's dick rubbing up and down my swollen lips, sensitive from his earlier ministrations. Gently he guides himself into my wet heat, thrusting slowly and deep as he pushes into the hilt. I let out a guttural moan, feeling filled to my limit by his sizable length.

Slowly he thrusts in and out of me, at an almost leisurely pace, the constant friction from his torturous speed building in my vagina, as his dick rubs along my g-spot at the perfect angle. The rhythm is so smooth and continuous that I'm sopping wet with need. The sound of our sex filling the space and turning me on like nothing else, knowing that Anton is watching us.

Keneth pants out in between thrusts directing his words to Anton, "Why don't you fuck her if you want her so badly, if you know she's yours then why are you resisting this?" Groaning as his body slaps hard against mine in slow, deep movements.

"Shut up and fuck her, Bear, don't you see she needs more, can't you smell her need. Slam into her and make her moan louder." Anton fires back, sounding frustrated.

Keneth continues at his pace, slow and steady and I can't stand it anymore, "Fuck me harder. Please!" Desperation and desire lacing every word, I need more.

"Why don't you give in?" Keneth asks Anton, ignoring my plea as he moves his hips in and out, maddening me, the grip of his good hand tight and punishing on my hip, the only indication that he needs more too.

A growl sounds, "I can't." Anton shouts back, "Fuck her! Do it, fuck her hard, fuck her for me." He sounds as feral as I feel, arching my back and all but mewling for more.

All of a sudden, Keneth starts to plow into me hard and fast, over and over again, and I grasp the table from the force. "Harder!" I hear Anton growl, "Fuck her harder!" And oh my Lord, he does.

He fucks me so hard that my teeth chatter and I can't catch my breath, every hard thrust makes me cry out louder and louder, my body coming apart at the seams, my very life unravelling as the pleasure hits me even harder. Screaming so loud that it echoes into the cave, Keneth leans over me and grabs my shoulder, slamming into me hard one last time, holding me in place as we both cum. Shaking and rolling my eyes into the back of my head, the ecstasy built so far up that coming down makes me delirious, an orgasm that seems to never end.

He collapses on me, breathing heavily, our sweat mingles and our heartbeats racing together as he lays on top of me and for a long while we don't move, we can't move. Our bodies need rest, even if just for a moment.

"Fucking hell that was hot." Breaks the silence and Keneth and I can't help it and start to softly laugh.

Standing back up and pulling me into his embrace, wearing the smile that I've come to adore, Keneth looks at Anton and smirks, "And to think you could've been involved too, sucks to be you." Before letting go of me and walking towards the bathroom, an obvious swagger to his step. "You coming, honey bee?" He throws back over his shoulder without looking back.

"I'll be there in a minute." I call after him, peering at Anton from under my lashes, "You need to have your wound looked at, I'm so sorry that I got distracted." I say sheepishly at Anton, still sitting naked in his chair, with a handful of cum.

He doesn't reply, just watches me quietly as I hand him the cloth from earlier to clean his hand with, and go to get a new one from the kitchen. "Let me wash you down and take care of you now, okay? No more distractions, I promise." I feel terrible that I let myself get sidetracked like that when Anton must be in a great amount of pain.

Smiling at me deviously as I come back he says, "You didn't seem to mind the distraction at the time."

"While that may be true, I should've put your needs first and taken care of this leg. How's it feeling?" I take a closer look at it. The injury, just like the other one, is healed at least a quarter of the way, which is astounding to look at but because it was such a large wound, there's still a lot of healing that needs to be done.

I wash him gently around the wound on his leg, and his baritone voice breaks my concentration, "Everything feels better when you're touching it, maybe a little higher would help, sweets," he adds as I get to the top part of his thigh, trying to ignore the penis dangerously close to my hand that starts to twitch back to life.

"No more distractions, Grizzly." I state and finish wiping down his body and cleaning his wound the best I can.

As I finish up, I stand and look him over, making sure I got every inch of him.

"You know there's something quite becoming of a female who hand washes my naked body, bare in front of me while smelling of sex and honey." Anton tilts his head to the side, staring blatantly at my tits and inhaling, "I could get used to this type of treatment."

"What are you doing, Anton?" My hands on my hips, one eyebrow raised, I can't help but wonder what his game is.

Looking up at me, feigning innocence he replies, "What do you mean?"

I raise my eyebrows even higher and place my hands on my hips, unashamed of my body, "You know what I mean. Why are you flirting with me? Masterbating over me? Staring at my naked body like you want to eat me for dinner? We both know that you don't want me in the long run, so what game are you playing at?" Crossing my arms over my chest, softening my face, I plead with him, "Please don't play me for a fool because I'm not one, and I don't appreciate you treating me that way. You realise that I have feelings, right?"

Inhaling and leaning his head back with his eyes closed he

replies, "I'm not trying to play with you, if you want me to keep my eyes and hands to myself I will, but you've got to understand that your body does things to me. I'm a male, in a sea of males, and you're a sexy breath of fresh air." Looking back up at me with soft eyes he speaks openly, "You're beautiful and your scent is like nothing I've ever tasted before, one whiff of it and it's on the tip of my tongue, making me salivate for more. I'll respect your wishes if you want me to back off though,"

Keneth comes strolling past us naked and clean from his shower, smelling amazing and fresh. "If you haven't figured out yet that she's your Kindred, then you don't deserve her." His voice completely nonchalant, like what he's saying is no big deal, "Go have a bath, honey bee, then come and snuggle with me." He walks straight into the bedroom without stopping or looking back.

Anton avoids my gaze when I look at him questioningly, so I turn and leave the room. Obviously Chuckles is wrong, because he doesn't seem to need me at all. Want me, sure but that's just because I'm just the first female in who knows how long that he's been able to touch and smell.

Walking into the bathroom, I decide not to think about it too much, or him. If I'm not careful I might catch feelings for Anton, and I'm just not willing to put myself through that, especially considering how lucky I am to have Keneth in my life, loving and accepting me unconditionally just the way I am.

As usual the water is the perfect temperature and I quickly submerge myself completely and let myself relax into the water, leaning my head against a rock and allowing my body to float softly, the heated liquid around me languidly lapping at my body from the ripple of the stream of the shower.

Looking up at the ceiling, I take in the soft rounded rock structure of the cave, I focus on the warm heat rising from the water into the air, and smell the soft clean scent of the fresh shampoo sitting next to my head.

Where does the water come from? I wonder, and where does it go? There's a constant flow of it falling from the roof in the corner but it never overflows and I find that curious. Nature is truly amazing, the way it works with us in the most unexpected ways.

Knowing that Keneth is waiting for me in bed, I slowly get myself out, after washing my body thoroughly. I dry myself and my hair as best I can, and head lazily back to the main room, passing Anton still naked in the chair.

He looks tired again, and I go to the kitchen and get some food and water for him, placing it on the small table at his side. I pick up his previously thrown blanket and carefully cover him, making sure he's tucked in comfortably. I would hate for him to get cold.

Taking both of my hands in his as I go to leave, Anton pulls me down to his face and kisses me softly on my lips, "Thank you for taking care of me, I know that you didn't have to and I appreciate it, female. No one has ever cared for me like this before and I don't want you to think that I'm not grateful, because I am." I feel my face flush with heat at his unusually soft words and actions.

I stroke his cheek, brushing his bristly skin lightly and look deep into his eyes, "Of course I'll take care of you, Anton, that's not even an option for me." I pause before continuing, "You can touch me as long as it's okay with Keneth, as soon as he isn't cool with it anymore, you stop. If I stupidly get feelings, then it will be my own fault."

Anton's brow furrows, "You could never get feelings for me anyway, we both know after everything I've done to you that I don't deserve it." Closing his eyes and letting me go he murmurs, "I'm unlovable."

"Never say never, my friend." I return, walking back into the bedroom and hopping into bed beside the already sleeping Keneth.

Before I close my eyes to sleep, I look out the bedroom door and find Anton staring at me, with a look that closely resembles longing in his bottomless eyes.

CHAPTER EIGHTEEN

"How are we going to get out of here exactly? Is there another way out?" Keneth asks Anton over breakfast. Both bears are looking a lot better this morning. Their healing ability blows my mind, never in a million years would I have ever expected to see someone with such horrific injuries heal at such a rapid rate.

Sighing deeply Anton replies, "Actually, no. It's an only one way in kind of deal, you know it's too risky to make dens with more than one entry. Can't have people sneaking in."

"You're not wrong but now we're pretty stuck, don't you think?" Keneth adds between chews.

"Hmmm..." Anton rubs his chin in thought, while my stomach flips at the thought of being permanently trapped here. All of a sudden, I'm feeling a little claustrophobic right now.

Noticing my rising discomfort, Keneth takes my hand into his and kisses each of my knuckles gently, smiling sweetly the whole time. "It'll be fine, don't stress. If worse comes to worst, we'll just pull one rock away at a time until we're free. No big deal."

"We'll have to wait until our injuries are healed though. I have enough food stored here for now and there's plenty of fresh running water." Anton adds, "It's just important that we're healthy in case there's a threat outside waiting for us. Gremlins are known for being persistant fucking things and the last thing we need is to go out there like this and be eaten alive." *That sounds reassuring.*

With shivers traveling down my spine at the thought of those *things,* I ask with a shudder, "Is that what they're called? Why were they after us? How come I haven't seen them or heard of them until now?"

Anton stops eating and leans back in his chair. "Sweets, we don't talk about Downworlders much if we can help it, it's considered bad luck in some circles. There are all sorts of things from down there but things like that only come up when a door's been left open too long by something of a higher tier. Not all of the Downworlder creatures are as primitive as Gremlins. While they're incredibly vicious and run in large packs, they don't have the same level of intelligence as Mhanu's. They're pretty much just driven by hunger and pain." Anton looks at Keneth, with something passing between them that makes my hackles rise before he continues, "It's the other things that you need to worry about, the smarter, larger things that go bump in the night."

Keneth adds with obvious trepidation, "What worries me, is that if the Gremlins are here, then something worse has had to have come through for them to be here." He squeezes my hand on the table, "That's another reason for us to stay inside for now, let's let whoever it is pass through without giving them a reason to focus on us."

Scrunching my face in confusion I ask, "What do you mean by '*whoever*'?" The choice of word, sends shivers traveling down my spine, not a *what* but a *who.*

Clearing his throat Anton answers, "Most likely it was a

Demon or Vampyre that opened the door. Let's just hope there's only one."

"Do you think they heard about the market?" Anton asks, absently rubbing his growing stubble.

Keneth growls in response at the reminder and I send him a warning look not to start anything because I don't want them fighting.

"Probably, only the worst kind of male would go there." Keneth mumbles under his breath, toning it down for me but still poking, the not so proverbial bear... "They probably want a female as a slave or maybe food."

"Most likely they want to procreate as well, plus they'd be just as desperate as any Mhanu or Angel to get their dicks wet." Anton replies, ignoring the growl and jab at him.

Keneth sits up straight at that. "You reckon?" Rubbing his face with his hand he asks, "What do you mean Angels? Do you really think that they'd be interested too? Fuck, if that's the case there'll be nothing stopping them from taking any female they wanted."

I chirp in. "When we met the Angel Ariel on the way here, he seemed sickeningly interested in getting a female pet." I say, scowling at the memory.

"You met Ariel?" Keneth asks, distinctly uncomfortable as he fidgets in his seat and frowns deeply at me.

Nodding, I get up and walk over to him, sitting gently in his lap, wrapping my arms around his neck, making sure not to touch his sore arm, and I give him a soft kiss, "Yeah, my dreams of what an Angel would be like, were very thoroughly dashed."

"Janice went straight up to him and was all 'save me'." Anton mimics my voice and shakes his head, "I thought he was going to take her for sure."

"You did what?" Keneth looks terrified by that, "Please stay away from the Angels, honey bee. They aren't a peaceful race, you don't want to be mixed up in all of that." He wraps his good arm around me and squeezes.

"So you guys are pretty much telling me that I need to stay away from Demons, Angels, and Vampyres. Oh, and that most Mhanu just want me as a pet to procreate with and abuse?" I ask incredulously, feeling super warmed by this topic... not.

"Yep, that about sums it up." Anton answers. "Welcome to Rathe, bet you're glad you stayed now." He smirks at me.

"I am actually." I stand up and walk out of the room saying as I leave, "I found love and hope here, and that's the most important thing. I'm going for a bath."

I hear two deep frustrated sighs and Keneth quietly saying, "She's not taking this seriously." But I am, I know the risks and I'm understandably frightened but I know that one way or another everything will work out because it always does.

* * *

Throwing my now dirty shirt on the floor of the bathroom, I wade smoothly into the big bath; this is definitely my favourite room in the house. I lower myself right into the deep end and put my head under the water for a moment, enjoying being totally enveloped. Water has a special way of making the whole world drift away, the depths soaking away all sound, all fears, and taking me to a place of pure peace and comfort. I've always had a love of water, ever since I was a kid.

My head breaks the surface again and I hear Keneth behind me on the stone floor, "I was worried that you were going to stay under there forever. Do you have gills that I don't know about like the Sirens do?"

I laugh lightly, "Sorry, I love the water. Are there really Sirens here or are you messing with me?" I ask, trying to remember if I've already been told this or not.

"Yep," he chuckles, "there sure are. They're the water element Fae and it's amazing what they can do with the water. They're pretty cool guys usually, unlike some of the other Fae, I'll take you to see them one day if you'd like?"

I smile up at him with a wide grin, "That'd be awesome. Are the Fae going to be at the markets too?" I'm curious about the types of people who would try to buy a woman, and I really don't know that much about anything here except for the shifters.

"Honestly, honey bee, there'll be a whole lot of different types of people there. I imagine that not all of them will be there for the wrong reasons. Some males might just be desperate for love or maybe even there to play the hero and save as many as he can." Joining me in the water he continues, "I know for a fact that there's a large amount of strong males hoping to save the females and packs that've pooled together their resources hoping to outbid the unworthy males, in order to save as many as they can but the problem is that there are so very many powerful males going with terrible intentions and a lot to barter with, that it'll be hard to save them all unfortunately."

Wrapping his big arm around me, I look up at him with love, "I'll be okay you know."

"What are you talking about? You can't honestly expect me to let you go to the markets just so that Anton can get laid." Frowning deeply at me, Keneth makes it clear where he stands.

Patting his cheek I reply, "Of course I do, because you won't hinder my free will. Will you?"

"It's out of the question, Janice!" His voice snaps like a rubber band.

"I'm not actually asking you, it's my life and I can decide this for myself." I'm irritated that he's telling me what to do, even though I understand why he's doing it.

Squeezing me tighter, Keneth rests his head on mine, "Please don't make me out to be the bad guy here, I'm just trying to protect you. What Anton's asking you to do is selfish and will put you in serious danger and I'm never going to be okay with that. I don't want to lose you, I've only just got you back."

I sigh in resignation of his point, "I know, darling, but it's ultimately my choice, he's not forcing me. I have to do the right thing. I have an opportunity to help him and it wouldn't be right if I just stood by and did nothing. He deserves better than that."

With hard eyes looking past me to the door, Keneth states, "No, he doesn't, but you do."

"He's right, sweets." I hear in Anton's deep voice that I can't help but to love, the sound sending shivers down my spine, "You shouldn't go to the market, it was wrong of me to expect you to in the first place. It makes me just as bad as the males willing to buy someone and if I stoop so low, then I truly don't deserve to get a Kindred of my own. I want to be worthy of my female."

I turn and gaze over to Anton leaning heavily in the doorway. "Your leg," I squeal, starting to get out of the bath at the same time that Anton puts his hand up to halt me.

"Stop, I'm fine. Stay in the bath." He says trying to stop my advance.

Ignoring him, I leave the water and lean my body under his arm, trying to take off some of the weight from his sore leg.

Anton sucks in a breath as I lean tight against him wet and naked, his arm over my shoulder, hand dangling close to my breast. Antons breathing becomes more shallow and I watch as his pupils dilate. Looking up at him, my own heart rate picks up at his reaction to me and our naked bodies flat against each other.

"I'm too heavy for you." His voice has a husky tone filled with unspoken need.

I squeeze him a bit harder, "And yet here I am."

A chuckle sounds from the bath and we both look over, snapped out of our momentary trance to see Keneth laughing in the bath, head back and filled with mirth.

"What's so funny, chuckles?" I feel lighter from his jovial laughter, and humour laces my voice.

Pointing at Antons rock hard dick he says, "This fucking guy. Yeah, Janice doesn't affect you at all, does she?" He continues laughing.

Anton's face flushes red, "The fuck man? Don't point at my dick."

"For the love of the Celestial's, just come to terms with the fact that you have a human Kindred, it's not like it's a bad thing anyway. She's hot as fuck, amazing in bed, and a worthy female that would risk her own life for your stupid ass." Shaking his head while breaking off his laughter, he finishes, "You couldn't do better if you tried."

Anton tenses next to me, so I try to lighten his mood before he gets angry at Keneth's teasing, "It's okay Keneth, leave him alone, I'm not what he's looking for and I've said in the past that it's fine. Don't make him uncomfortable by trying to force me onto him." I pull at Anton, "Come on let's see if we can get you in the bath since you're up and about."

Changing the subject seems to work because he starts to limp toward the bath, not putting too much pressure on me.

Very carefully we get him into the water, Keneth helps to guide him down as well. Anton's such a strong male, even as the water covers his injured leg, he doesn't flinch. I know his pain must be incredible at the moment, but Anton refuses to let it show. I've never known a man like him before. Mind you, Keneth has been just as brave in his rapid recovery.

"Are you alright?" I ask, worried about how he's feeling and not wanting to push him too far, too fast.

After settling back against the side, sitting on a makeshift stone seat with the water up to mid-chest, Anton replies tensely, "I'm fine."

"Let me wash you down and take care of you." I get the soap from the side without waiting for his response because I'm not asking. Keneth sits back under the shower spray coming from the roof, relaxing and watching us appearing calm and unfazed and unfazed.

Lifting one of Anton's arms up, I lather it with soap, washing it thoroughly from his shoulders all the way down to his finger tips. Antons eyes are on me the whole time, watching me with something akin to disbelief and awe.

Suddenly, he lifts his other hand and puts a strand of hair that's fallen in front of my face behind my ear, then strokes the back of it softly down my cheek, stopping at my chin and taking it into his grasp. Lifting my face to look at him while his eyes bore into mine. "Thank you, for being you, my sweets."

He said *my* and it brings a flutter to my heart, as if butterflies were unleashed in my chest at the endearment. I know it probably doesn't mean anything, but I can't help but react to him, wishing that it was so.

"You're so beautiful and kind and Keneth is lucky to have you as a Kindred." He takes his hand back and my heart deflates just a little bit when he does. I knew it was too good to be true. I have to remember to be careful not to get my hopes up. He's always been clear with where he stands with me.

My disappointment must have shown on my face because Keneth wades over to us and pulls me into his arms and away from

Anton. "I *am* the luckiest male in all of the worlds, honey bee, there's no one in *any* world that I would ever want above you. I'll never look at another female but you ever again, you are my world and I'll make you feel loved every day of our lives. I'll never ever let you down or hurt you, I promise."

I know he's trying to cheer me up but I can also hear the underlying accusation that he's throwing at Anton for not claiming me as his own. It's sweet that he places my happiness above any sort of jealousy or competition that could crop up. Keneth's sole desire is to just make me happy and keep me safe. It warms my heart back up and reminds me that I don't need Anton's acceptance when I have this perfect man before me.

Placing a kiss on his cheek I say meaningfully, "Thank you, my darling. I know that and I feel the same about you. I'm sorry if I haven't shown you enough."

"Don't be sorry, you've been amazing. You've taken such good care of me and this idiot and we appreciate it." A genuine smile lights up his handsome features, bright blue eyes twinkling with the love he feels for me.

"Who are you calling an idiot?" Anton says and I remember that I was meant to be washing him. These two are so distracting.

"If it looks like an idiot and sounds like an idiot, then there's a good chance it's an idiot." Keneth chuckles.

"Fuck off." Anton snaps back, flipping him the bird.

I laugh, going back to Anton and lifting his other arm to clean. "You two stop it." I snicker.

Rubbing his arm up and down, I go up to his chest and start smoothing my hands over his thick bulging shoulder muscles and sculpted chest. I swallow hard, enjoying the feel of all of his taut plains under my fingertips. I accidentally moan as I circle his lower abdomen, red flushes my cheeks and I pull my hands back in embarrassment.

With a deep rumble Anton says, "Don't stop now, sweets, I have plenty more for you to rub." Taking my hands back and he places them on his chest and slides them slowly down and over his well developed eight pack, all the way down to cover his thick, pulsing cock.

I gasp as I make contact with it, the hot silky feel of his flesh heats up in my hand and I can't help but to grasp it tightly and stroke the full impressive length. I think about how good it would feel, filling up my pussy and I shiver.

"Keep going, don't stop." He pulls me closer and in between his legs.

I look back at Keneth for approval and see him watching us with hooded eyes, he gives me a small nod telling me that it's alright and he wades towards us. I turn back and stroke Anton again, getting rewarded with a moan from his parted lips and his head falls back in pleasure. A big hand coming from behind me moulds to my small breast and rubs a calloused palm on my now aching nipple.

My other hand reaches lower and cups Anton's heavy sack, kneading it gently as I continue stroking his length, all the while my nipple is teased and tingling from Keneth's ministrations, my pussy clenching in response.

Keneth places his big body flush against mine, his hard member pushing against my back until he lowers himself slightly, slipping his dick in between my legs, so that it rubs against my core. Back and forth he rolls his hips, friction builds against my clit, my legs closed and tight around his cock, strong thighs clasping it there and making me a whole different kind of wet.

I squeeze and stroke Anton just how he likes it, tight and slow, bending over toward him slightly. Keneth pushes his cock at my centre as I open my legs slightly for him, slowly he thrusts his way inside me, bit by bit filling me. Anton, unable to just sit there taking the pleasure I'm building in him, pulls my head in to kiss me passionately, his tongue devouring my mouth, while his other hand lowers to thrum my clit as Keneth thrusts inside me all the way.

Moaning deeply, I move my hips with his rhythm, loving having him inside me and wishing that I could have them both.

"Yes," I cry out in Anton's mouth, the movement from the two of them pulling me closer to climax, having one in front of me and one behind is so hot, the visual almost as good as the feeling. My mouth still on Anton I cry out again, "Fuck, yes."

Anton pants as I keep stroking him, faster and faster, gripping my hair with one hand and rolling my clit with his other. "Cum for me, sweets!" He growls in my mouth, and then I do as if on command, coming apart around Keneth's dick as he continues to thrust hard inside me.

"Fuck me!" I scream, and I get pounded even harder from behind.

Anton grabs my hand to stop me from making him cum and says in a deep husky tone, "Turn around." It's an order, not a request.

Surprisingly, Keneth pulls out of me and turns me around, backing me into Antons lap and swiftly filling me again, pulling my legs up and around his waist. Keneth takes my mouth for a demanding kiss and begins to pump into me again, only slower.

I feel Antons finger suddenly at my behind, probing my hole gently, rubbing it and making my pussy clench at how surprisingly good it feels. Then he pushes one finger inside me, moving it in and out in time with Keneth's thrusts. Moaning deeply, I move my hips more, loving the feeling and he inserts a second finger, stretching my ass to accommodate it. I never knew that this could feel so good.

Just when I think I'm going to cum again, Anton takes his

fingers out of me and I feel so empty, wanting them back inside me. I feel the head of Antons penis suddenly pushing against my behind and gently squeezing inside my hole, I arch my back slightly and Keneth keeps his hips still, reaching down between us and strokes my nub, rubbing it and pinching it as Anton slides his big dick deeper inside me, filling me up in a way that makes me gasp out for air. The slight pain mixing with the overwhelming pleasure builds up inside me. I throw my head back screaming "Yes!", as he reaches all the way to his hilt. Two big cocks, loaded inside me and still for a moment to let me accommodate my body to the fullness.

Slowly, Keneth starts to move inside me again, still stroking my clit. The two of them begin fucking me in both holes with a perfect rythm that has me clenching and moaning in pleasure. Within minutes I scream out my orgasm again and again, the overwhelming sensation of being thoroughly fucked by both of them is incredible.

Quickening their thrusts and really pounding into me now, they both start to pant heavily and I can feel them growing even harder inside me as they thrust hard together, Anton using his arm strength and Keneth punishing me with his powerful hips. Anton pulls my hair so hard that my head falls back onto him and he growls into my ear, "Cum again, sweets, cum while we fill you." He nips at my ear letting go of my hair and moves his hand around to strum my clit instead. I stay leaning back on Anton, and Keneth leans down and bites my taught nipple hard, pushing me over the edge again, my pussy and ass clench them tight as I violently cum in a rush, feeling both men tense and groan almost simultaneously as they fill me with their seed.

"Fuuuuck." Anton moans into my neck, trembling as he comes down from the high of our shared orgasm. "You're so fucking hot." He nips me gently before kissing me all the way up to my ear, taking my earlobe into his mouth and sucking on it, sending shivers down my spine.

Keneth sucks and licks both of my nipples gently as my body relaxes, savouring them with his mouth, both of them still deep inside me. I sigh in pleasure, feeling amazing and also really tired. I close my eyes and smile showing my contentment while leaning comfortably against Anton's hard body, enjoying them both so close to me, feeling better than I ever have. The moment, rare, and perfect.

CHAPTER NINETEEN

Waking up I instantly feel ill, the room smells super rotten, filling my mouth with saliva when I breathe it in further and my eyes snap open with the sudden recognition... sulfur.

I sit straight up immediately aware that I'm alone in bed, the previous night's activities take over my mind for a moment and I can't help the warm feeling that tingles throughout my body at the memory of both Anton and Keneth inside me. *I can't believe I did that.*

Muffled voices trickle through the doorway, bringing me back to the present situation. The guys must be out and about, talking low thinking that I'm still asleep. I move my feet to the floor and look around for something to wear. Screw it, they've seen it all before, I'm confident with my body, I don't see why I should cover up now.

Padding lightly over to the door I stick my head around the corner, being as quiet as I can because I want to hear what they're saying so quietly. I know I shouldn't snoop but I'm sure they're being quiet for a reason.

"I don't see how we're gonna be able to hide this from her?" I hear Keneth say, "It's probably best if we're honest."

"Are you kidding me right now? The last thing she needs is to freak out over this shit. Don't you think she's been through enough?" Anton whisper-yells back, "She took care of us for Celestial knows how long before we came to again, and all on her own, and she's still doing so much to help us mend, the least we can do is to protect her from this."

Keneth's voice raises slightly, "Protect her! Are you serious? You were going to fucking sell her! You don't have a fucking right to tell me about protecting her." I tip toe closer so that I can see them around the corner, their body language is clearly tense and they're in each other's faces, with Keneth pointing his index finger into Antons huge pecs.

Anton pushes Keneths hand away and says through gritted teeth, "Don't fucking touch me, *Chuckles*, or I'll break that finger off your fucking hand, you know I'm right. We need to come up with a valid reason for what's happening and we need to do it fast, before she wakes up."

"Janice won't appreciate being lied to, it's a bad idea!" Keneth snaps back.

I step forward and into their eye view, "Darn straight I won't like it, you'd better tell me right now what's going on before *I* become your biggest problem." I say to them, with my head held high and my hands on my hips, "And don't even try to sweet talk me."

They both turn to me, clearly shocked that I'm standing there and I watch amused, as their gazes go from defensive to heated, travelling down my naked body from head to toe and back again.

I'm obviously a distraction and I snap my fingers to get their attention again.

"My eyes are up here," I point to my face, "What are you trying to hide from me? Focus!" I snap the last word, showing them that I'm serious.

They look at each other and then back at me, neither of them wanting to be the person to tell me what's going on. Shuffling their feet and looking distinctly uncomfortable Keneth starts, "There's been a development, honey bee. It seems that the Gremlins are still outside."

Clearing his throat Anton adds, "Actually, it's a bit worse than that, we've been hearing the rocks shuffling on the other side of the collapse, and we're pretty sure they're digging their way to us down the tunnel. Seems we're still on the menu."

Keneth nudges Anton hard in the side before telling him, "Did you have to add that? You could be a bit nicer about it, you know."

"Hey, you're the one that wanted to tell her the truth, there's no sugar coating the fact that they want to eat us!" Anton defends, gruffly.

I just stand there taking in everything that they've said. The Gremlins are coming and there's no way out! What am I supposed to do with that? My body decides that hyperventilating is the way to go and before I know it my hands are on my knees and I'm struggling for breath, my chest tight and sweat beginning to coat me in my panic.

"Fuck, sweets!" Anton hobbles over to where I'm having my mini meltdown, my mind flashes to those creatures' large mouths and sharp teeth dripping with blood. I begin shaking uncontrollably, my mind working overtime with horrific scenes of them eating my insides.

Both men surround me, rubbing my back and whispering things that are meant to calm me but I can't hear anything through the pounding of my own heart. I'm hoisted over someone's shoulder, vaguely conscious that it's Keneth that has a hold of me by his delicious scent of maple tree, berries and cinnamon. Not before long I'm submerged in the stone bath, with the shower drizzling over my head bringing me back to awareness.

"Son of a gun," I murmur against the strong shoulder that my head's leaning on, "what are we gonna do?" and with that, I start to cry. One strong arm envelops me from the front as Anton gently begins to stroke my hair from behind, moving it to the side and kissing me gently on the nape of my neck.

"It'll be alright, sweets, we'll figure it out, we won't let them hurt you, baby." Anton whispers sweetly in my ear and I continue to cry my fear out in the bath with Keneth trying to squeeze all my terror away.

I stay like that for some time before I run out of tears to cry. I lean back onto Anton, after wrapping my legs around Keneth, and I know without a doubt that if they can, these two males will save me and I need to get myself together because right now we're a team; I can't let them down.

"Do you guys have a plan?" My voice is hoarse from crying.

With a deep sigh Anton replies, "Not yet but we will. They're still a ways off yet, so we have time. Don't worry, we've got this."

"I know." I hop down and scoot away from them, turning in the water to face them both head on, "Let's figure this out. Are you sure there's no other way out of here, Grizzly?"

He shakes his head, "Nope, definitely not."

"Okay, well maybe we can fight them as they come through, if they only have enough room to come in one at a time then we should be able to manage it. Have you got any weapons we can use?" I'm trying really hard to find a silver lining here.

"It's not that simple, they're like carnivorous cockroaches, they'll come in so quickly that we'll be swarmed in minutes and they're very hard to kill, love." Keneth says to me gently, obviously worried about how I'm going to take that news but I'm done crying; I need to focus and live. "It'd be near impossible to defeat them." He finishes, being brutally honest with me.

"There has to be something we can do?" I ask them but they just shrug their shoulders, looking defeated.

"Why don't we go and have something to eat and think about it for a while, I'm sure we'll come up with something between the three of us." Anton says as he moves to get out of the bath.

Keneth nods, "Good idea, I'm starving anyway. There's no such thing as any great plans on an empty stomach."

"I'll meet you guys out there, I'm going to relax here for a bit, I'm not hungry right now anyway." My nerves flitter in my stomach and I need to be alone.

Keneth leans over to kiss me sweetly on the cheek as he joins Anton, both of them moving off together as I marvel at their healing bodies. It's astonishing.

Leaning back and letting my body float, I close my eyes and focus on the sound of the trickling water as it hits the bath and let calmness envelop me. Feeling one with the water I concentrate on how the warm water feels on my skin, the soft mist of the shower coating me and letting myself slowly float until my head lightly taps against the wall. Opening my eyes I notice that I've moved right to the other end of the bath, the light current sweeping me away from the flow of water from the roof.

I look over to where it begins to trickle down, the hole that it comes from is no bigger than the width of my calf, there's no way we can get through there. If only it was wider, if only it was a way out of this place.

Wait a minute! An idea forms in my head, where does the water go from here? Standing up I gaze down into the water, it's hard to see into the depths from down this end because the sole light is at the other side of the room. I let my hands run across the smooth rock wall behind me before I duck my head down under the surface of the water, feeling with my hands as I go. I do this several times and it isn't until I get to the darkest corner that I feel give way under my feet, the slight dip in the floor noticeable now that I'm looking for it. Sinking down under the water once more, I follow the wall until it disappears, curving away from me, a gentle pull to the water at the entrance, coaxing me further into the hole that feels big enough to make me panic a little at the idea of getting stuck down here.

Rising to the surface I call out, "Guys come and see! I think I found something."

Excitement fills me at the possibility of finally getting out of this den.

CHAPTER TWENTY

Only seconds pass before both Anton and Keneth are at the pool entrance looking over to me in confusion as I smile at them, my grin large and animated, "There's a water tunnel. Do you have a portable light?"

"What do you mean there's a water tunnel? I think I'd know something like that." Anton replies skeptically.

Shaking my head at him I reply, "Guess you don't know everything then. Why did you think the bath never overflowed?"

Eyes wide open, he looks at me shocked. "How did I never think of that?"

"Because you're clearly an idiot." Keneth snaps at him.

With a quick laugh I say, "You shouldn't be too quick to judge, you never thought of it either, did you?"

"I would have." He smiles back at me mischievously.

"Mmm hmm, sure you would've." I laugh again, feeling light and optimistic. "So, Grizzly, do you have a light or something so we can see what it looks like? It's way too dark down there to see."

Hobbling off he calls back, “Yeah I’ll go and get a couple of mini spheres, I always have extras handy.”

Keneth wades into the water where I’m waiting, “Where is it?”

I point down, “Near my feet and to the left a bit I think.”

He pops under the water in the direction I pointed at the same time that Anton comes back in with three spheres in his hands. Slowly he lowers himself down to us being careful with his injured leg, “Even if there’s a decent sized hole, we aren’t fish. You do know that right? We can’t breathe underwater and we have no idea how long that hole will go back.”

Taking a sphere from him I reply, “I’m aware of that but do you have a better plan we can work with because I’m all ears if you do?” He just stares at me, “I didn’t think so.” My voice smug.

Keneth breaks the surface and asks for a sphere of his own. “That’s actually a decent size hole, I’ll have another look with this and see how far I can swim down.”

“That’s a bad idea.” Anton snaps. “What if you run out of air or get stuck or something?”

I purse my lips and frown, “He has a point, maybe we should tie a rope around your ankle or something and you can pull on it if you need us to pull you back or we can do it if you take too long down there. What do you think?”

“I have some long rope under my bed.” Anton replies.

I swim away and out of the bath as quickly as I can so that I don’t have to deal with any objection from Keneth. Making my way briskly into the bedroom dripping water all over the floor, I pop down under the bed and find the rope immediately. Grabbing it, I race back to the bathroom and throw it over to Anton who catches it with fast reflexes.

“Start tying him up.” I say.

Laughing hard Keneth says, “You’d like that wouldn’t you, honey bee? No need to demand it, you can tie me up anytime.”

Anton and Keneth fist bump and chuckle away together, it warms my heart seeing the two of them laughing and getting along together for a change. It makes me almost want to daydream about a world where we can all be together but I know that it's just a fantasy and it'll never be a reality for me. Anton has made his view about Kindreds very clear, and I'm not it.

Snapping out of my mini reverie, I sit on the side of the bath closest to where they are, watching as Anton straps up Keneth's ankle and makes sure that it's secure.

"Right, I'm ready." Looking over at me Keneth says, "Don't worry, my love, I'll be right back. Piece of cake." Before I can answer him, he took a deep breath and dived under the water.

"You have the other end right?" I ask Anton, needing reassurance.

Holding his hands up to show me the rope gently sliding through his fingers as he smiles, "It's all good, I've got him."

The room goes deathly quiet, except for the trickling of the shower behind us, we both watch the rope gliding between his fingers at a steady rate, time seeming to slow, ticking by at an alarming rate for my panicking heart that thumps forcefully in my chest. Bubbles randomly seep to the surface of the water, reminding me of every breath he isn't taking, it's been too long, what if something happens to him? It'll be all my fault.

"This was a terrible idea, pull him out, he's gonna drown." I almost shout at Anton when I can't stand the wait any longer. "Please, pull him out!" My voice rose in panic.

"Trust him, sweets, he'll come back when he can't swim anymore."

"No. It'll be too late by then, he has a bad arm, why didn't we think of his arm?" I insist, dropping my body into the water and wading over to him in a flurry, splashing water around as I go.

I look down into the water, desperate for a sign of his light, desperate for a sign of anything. I lower myself into the water with my sphere facing the hole and see something in the dark swimming up to me, fast. Jumping up I yell, "Pull!"

Anton doesn't question me this time, he just grabs a hold of the rope and pulls as hard and fast as he can, while I go back under and keep my sphere lowered near the entrance. With one last heave Keneth breaks through the hole and we both jump to the surface with a huge outward splash, he gulps in air furiously and breathes hard and fast to catch his breath.

Jumping on him in utter relief I cry out his name. "Oh my gosh, I thought I'd lost you, you were gone for so long."

"Let him catch his breath, female." Anton says as he pries me off my Kindred. "You're gonna suffocate him." I turn and wrap myself around Anton instead, needing to feel grounded.

"I'm sorry, my darling, I didn't mean to." I cry back at Keneth, feeling terrible about accosting him. "Are you okay?"

Coughing a little bit but gaining air again Keneth replies in between gasps, "I'm fine, honey bee, I just needed a little oxygen." He manages a smile.

Just then I realise how close I am to Anton when his dick twitches at my core while his large hands squeeze my behind, pulling me closer to rub against me. "Hey, none of that, Mr Bear." I slide back down his body.

"Sorry, sweets, can you blame me? You were pressed right against it with your heat and rubbing me." Reaching his arms around me he leans down for one more squeeze, pushing my body flush against his. "Plus, you feel amazing, and you know how much I love this ass."

Feeling my face go beet red at the memories of the night before, I extricate myself from his embrace and back up towards Keneth. "Um... yes." Is all my brain can manage apparently, both the guys start laughing at my obvious discomfort. "Oh shush, you two. What did you find, Chuckles? Is there hope?"

Keneth stops laughing almost immediately. *That's not a good sign.* "I swam as far as I could before I thought I might be in danger of drowning, I dropped my sphere at that point so that we can use it as a marker." He starts, "It's an easy enough width to swim through, if anything it gets wider in some sections but there were a few corners and I think there was a part that got deeper, it felt like the ground sloped down. It makes me a little nervous knowing that anything from down there can swim up here. Have you never had any creatures in here?" He asks, turning his attention to Anton.

"Nope, not that I've seen."

Frowning deeply Keneth continues, "I didn't see an end or any light that wasn't my own, I have no idea how much longer it goes on for or if we can even get out at the end. I think that one of us would have to swim all the way until they ran out of oxygen to find out if it's possible but that's a huge risk. Whoever goes would most probably just die in there trying to find their way out, it's not worth it in my opinion and it's a real mindfuck wondering if you're gonna make it back on time, I almost started to panic at the end until I saw your light, Janice, it's what kept me swimming."

"I knew it, you could have died and it would've been my fault." My heart pounds in my chest at how close I got to losing him again. "I wouldn't have been able to live with myself if something happened to you."

"Sweets, if he'd died you wouldn't be living at all, remember. I should've gone instead, we risked both of your lives." Anton says with frustration lacing his voice.

Looking at me sharply Keneth snaps, "Holy Celestials, you're right. What was I thinking? I'm so sorry, honey bee." Coming over to me, he embraces me tightly as if he's scared to let me go. "I never wanted to risk your life, my Kindred, not ever."

"It's still our best bet though at the moment, if it comes down to it then I'll go." Anton starts, raising his hand to halt my pending argument. "No, Janice, I'm not saying I'll try it right now, but it needs to be said as a backup plan in case we can't come up with a better idea. For now though, I think we'll be fine for another day, maybe two. They're not the smartest creatures and they have a whole lot of rock carnage to get through before they'll reach us. As it is, it'll probably collapse on them a few times on their way through it. It's been said now, so let's move on to any other ideas we can come up with, no arguments." His hand is raised for effect, and his face, stone.

Exiting the water, Anton moves to the towel to dry himself off, turning to me he asks, "Do you want another one of my shirts to wear or are you putting your other clothes on? I noticed that they were clean and hanging up."

"Do you mind if I borrow another one? They're so comfy." I say with a small smile, following him out.

Winking at me, Anton throws me the towel, "Of course, sweets, anytime. I want you to be comfortable, plus you look hot as fuck in them, especially when you bend over."

"Hey, hey, hey. What about me?" Keneth asks with humour.

"Don't worry, darling, you look good when you bend over too." I flutter my lashes at him.

Laughing hard we all dry ourselves and Anton turns to Keneth, "Giving you clothes was a given, I'm sick of seeing your fucking cock every time I turn around, it's not okay dude."

"You're just jealous that my dick's bigger than yours."

"Fuck off it is." Anton snaps back, "Are you blind or just stupid?"

Stepping between them with my arms stretched out and a shit

eating grin I get involved, "Now, now cubs, you're both very big and macho, but it's obvious that I have the biggest dick here."

Winding up the towel, Keneth snaps it on my bare bum, hard. "Ouch," I shout, running out of the bathroom and into the bedroom with both of them hot on my heels. Laughing heartily, I round the bed and jump over it before they can catch me and sprint back towards the door before being grabbed from behind and lifted off the ground with a squeal.

CHAPTER TWENTY-ONE

I stand alone in the dark with only the sphere in my hand to light my way, gazing numbly at the tumbled stone wall that happens to be the only object between us and the beasts beyond it. The burning tang of sulfur fills my nose and makes me cringe, the scent is so strong that I can taste it on my tongue, reminding me of how close I am to the possible end of my mortality. I shiver at the thought and hear mumbles of scraping and scratching from the Gremlins attempting to reach us. *Can they smell my fear? Do they know I'm here?*

I jump and squeal in terror as a heavy hand lands on my shoulder, spinning around to see a shocked Keneth, his arms now above his head in a show of submission.

"Honey bee, I didn't mean to frighten you." He whispers, concern written all over his face as my light shines off his chiseled features. "Why are you out here? It's not safe. Please come back to the den." Keneth holds out his arm for me to take, his voice low and almost a whisper.

"Are they getting closer or is it just me being paranoid?" I take his hand with my shaking one and we walk down the tunnel together like that. "I'm scared, Keneth." I admit, and even I can hear the wavering of my voice.

He pulls me under his arm for the rest of the way, squeezing me tight but remaining silent because we both know that there's nothing he can say, this is our reality at the moment and none of us have figured a way out of it.

When we stroll into the main living area of the den, I can't help but think about how being eaten alive has to be the worst way to die, and I can't stand here and find out. I let go of Keneth and go to sit next to Anton at the table. I look up at him and automatically want to kiss his cheek, but I know that he's funny about our situation. I'm never quite sure where I stand with him. Earlier we all had a great laugh and rumble in bed, but when it came time for anything more than that, he excused himself and hobbled out of the room, leaving Keneth and myself to do our own thing. All I seem to get from him are mixed messages, one minute he's in my behind, holding me tight and making me feel desired, and the next he's avoiding touching or looking at me altogether. Perhaps he feels like he's cheating on his Kindred and if that's the case then I don't want to push him, over time Anton has become, if nothing else, my friend.

"Chuckles darlin', can you sit down, I want to talk to you both." I start while fidgeting in my seat, knowing that what I have to say, neither of them are going to like.

Keneth sits down with a big smile that shines just for me, "Yes, my delicious honey bee."

Screwing his face up in a show of discomfort, Anton scoffs, "You guys can cut that shit out, it's fucking gross."

"Don't act like you don't think she's delicious." Keneth stirs with a smirk, “I’ve seen the way you lick your fingers savouring her juices like a starving man.”

“Fuck off, Bear,” Anton replies with the middle finger salute.

I bang my hand lightly on the table between them to gain their attention. “Are you two done?” I sigh, rolling my eyes. “This is serious.”

Anton clears his throat before mumbling, “Sorry Sweets, what’s wrong?”

They both turn their completely different gazes on me, Chuckles with his twinkling sapphire eyes, and Anton with his deep brown eyes, bore into mine.

I don’t know how to bring it up with any suave so I just go for it, “I think we should swim out.”

The room is quiet for a minute while I look down at my hands as I pick at my fingernails, avoiding the stares that I feel burning a hole into me from both sides. As the silence reigns on for even longer I stammer out, “I don’t want to get eaten, I know it’s risky and that we could drown, but to be honest I’d rather die like that, fighting to live, than being eaten alive. I can’t bear the thought, and I get nightmares every night about it.” I stop to catch my breath, not really sure when I started holding it to begin with.

A large hand slides over my now trembling hands and squeezes them still. “Honey bee, we won't let you be eaten. I don’t want you to worry about it, okay? Let us protect you and take care of you, everything will be alright. As your Kindred, I swear to do everything in my power to get you out of here in one piece.” I slowly look up at Keneth as one fat tear silently slides down my cheek, letting my fear show.

I’ve been holding it in and trying to pretend it’s not there for as long as I can but hearing those things scratching away at our stone confines, inching ever closer has made me face the reality of our situation, and I’m petrified.

With a slap on the table that makes me jump, Anton says, "It's way too soon for you to worry about it, and besides they could give up and go home yet. There's no need for a suicide mission." He gets up and hobbles over to the fridge, his leg wound has now completely filled back in and the skin around the area is the only thing left to heal.

I marvel at the sight as I watch him move around, taking in his shirtless back when he turns around to only see the scars left behind from the deep scratch marks he sustained in the fight with the Gremlins. It blows my mind that it was just over a week ago and both males look as though it's been months.

"Getting a good look, sweets?" Anton speaks as he bends over to get something from the bottom shelf of his cupboard. I blink rapidly at his words, cheeks heating at being caught looking at him, even though it really was only clinically.

Keneth chuckles his buoyant laugh that I love. "Leave her alone, you've made her change colour."

"Shush, the both of you. I was just looking at his injuries, honestly." I implore, pointing to Anton's back.

Coming back over Anton winks and hides a smile as he sits down with a can of fruit and Keneth laughs again, "Of course you were, honey bee." His tone clearly mocks me for his amusement.

Getting up, I turn around and walk towards the bedroom leaving their combined laughter behind, when I get to the doorway I look at them with my hand on my popped out hip, "Son of a gun, how do I deal with the two of you? It's a surprise I haven't lost my faculties." Their laughter just increases and when I turn my head away from them I can't help the smile that lines my lips from hearing their happiness.

* * *

I MUST HAVE FALLEN asleep reading a book 'Human Interactions' that I found in the bookcase here when I get woken up by hard thumping and bangs in one of the other rooms, I lift my head and rub sleep away from my eyes as I see Anton running past the bedroom door in a mighty hurry, the loud thumping of his feet hitting the floor, the reason I must have woken. *Where is he going in such a hurry?*

More banging of a different kind sounds off down the tunnel, along with raised voices of panic, making my hackles rise and I'm wide awake in seconds, placing my feet on the ground and warily head out the door to see what's going on that has the males so riled up.

Screeching noises of something being dragged and a hard thump reverberate around the tunnel as I get closer to the commotion, the rancid stench of rotten eggs is so thick in the air now, that it makes me dry retch from being in the vicinity.

Scratch! Scratch! Scratch!

The sound of Gremlins claw away at our only means of escape, filling my ears loud and clear, closer than I ever dared to imagine. Suddenly, a terrifying screech bursts down the tunnel and I feel the noise in my bones and I take a moment to pray that we'll get through this... somehow.

I make my feet keep moving and my legs tremble beneath me with each step until I turn the corner and see what Anton and Keneth are doing. Just as I turn it, Anton is in front of me, I scream out in surprise and he visibly jumps back, clearly just as shocked as I was. Which goes to show how distracted he must be.

Catching his breath as he pants he asks anxiously, "Why are you awake?"

"Are you kidding me? With the banging and the elephant man running by the bedroom, as if I'd still be asleep." I look past him at the slightly shivering wall. "What's happening? Are they getting through? Tell me the truth." My voice rises with an air of hysteria and I grip at his pants at the waist.

He grabs my shoulders forcefully, "Get your shit together. Breathe, female." His eyes bore into mine demanding that I listen.

I lean myself forward and rest my head on his hard, sweaty chest. I inhale and exhale, trying to calm myself down as I breathe in his heady scent of leather and wood. In a surprise move he lifts his hand and strokes my hair down tenderly, then lifts my chin so that I can look up to him.

"Good girl. Now stay calm because I'm not going to lie to you and this is going to be hard to hear." I nod my affirmative at him, concentrating on my breathing and letting myself get slightly lost in the smell of him. "They're here now, they're breaking through as we speak. Keneth and I have covered as many heavy things that we can over the entrance to slow them down but at this point..." he sighs deeply and leans his head onto mine, "There's no point. There's nothing we can do, sweets, I'm so sorry I couldn't keep you safe."

"Fuck that." Keneth booms loudly from behind as he approaches us, "I'll fight them all if I have to, I promised you that I'd keep you safe and I will. When we distract them, I want you to run. Between the two of us we might be able to hold them off long enough for you to find a new hiding place. You'll live, honey bee. You have to."

Keneth puts his arm around my back while my head leans on Anton's and Anton let's go of me and pulls Keneth in tighter and slaps him on the shoulder as a show of comradery.

"My friend," Anton starts as he lifts his head and looks at him over me, "if you die, she dies." A simple statement; true, direct and unavoidable.

I hear Keneth push out a shaky breath before they sandwich me between them, encompassing me in their bodies, their heat and scents surrounding me as our chests rise and fall, taking in the moment between us and coming to terms with our fate.

We die here today. Together.

CHAPTER TWENTY-TWO

A chair tumbles to the ground breaking our shared moment, and we look over together to see a long, claw tipped arm reaching through a hole in the rocks, grasping and grabbing things within arms reach and throwing it out of the way. The walls shake harder as the beasts increase their attack on it, knowing that dinner is just within reach, the sounds of their excitement and frenzy jolting me to action.

"Quick!" I clasp my hands with theirs and start to run, the two of them holding tight and following me as we pound through the caves. I run straight into the bathroom and Keneth halts, pulling me back, the shock of it almost making me fall over but Anton catches me in time.

Keneth tightens his grip on me, "No!" He booms, fear written on his tight features for the first time so far. "I'm not drowning you."

"Let me go, Keneth, we don't have time for this, they're going to get through that barricade at any moment. We need to go, we need to try." I urge, peeling his hand off mine. "I've always been able to hold my breath for a long time, you saw that for yourself, remember. You need to let me try to live!" I scream out and he pales. I know I'm panicking and that he doesn't deserve me snapping at him but I am desperate, my heart is pounding in my chest at a million miles an hour. I can't give up. I will get out of here, even if it means I die trying.

I hear sploshing and I turn to see Anton wading into the water towards the hole, "Let's go, Bear. You go first and I'll tie the rope to you, and connect it to her wrist, then if she's struggling you can pull her the rest of the way through." Anton rushes, waving us over. "I have to go last, with my leg, I'll only slow you two down. Come on, move it."

I jump in and join him as quickly as I can, Keneth now hot on my heels. "Let's do this. Promise me you'll be right behind me, Grizzly. I might need you to help me through too." I say to encourage him to follow me and not stay to be the hero.

He looks down at me with his usual serious face. "You're very conniving, Miss Sweets, do you know that?" I smile at him and reach up on my toes to give him a quick soft kiss on the cheek. "Smart too. Alright, I'll make sure you don't fall behind." He reaches over to the edge of the bath and grabs two spheres, handing one to Keneth.

A loud smash sounds off from the tunnel and my heart rate speeds up even more and I didn't know that was even possible at this point.

"Time to go." Keneth grabs my wrist and ties a rope tightly to it at the same time that Anton secures one around his waist. "Done, honey bee." Leaning forward he takes my face in his hands and kisses me hard, the kind of kiss that says a million words in only seconds, one that speaks of love, loss, fear, and devotion. A kiss that says goodbye.

I look up at him with tears in my eyes and turn to see Anton's expression of pain. Just as I go to give the same kind of kiss to him, to let him know that he's not alone in the world, the tunnel is filled with a myriad of sounds; scampering feet, scratching, bangs and the unmistakable sound of Gremlins closing in.

"Hold your breath." Anton whispers as Keneth disappears into the depths, "Go and *live*."

Inhaling as deep as I can, I dive into the water and push myself off the stone floor and into the depths of the unknown, following the light beyond me that Keneth holds as he swims, a beacon of hope as I swim as hard and fast as I can, never looking back but not doubting that Anton's behind me somewhere.

At first confidence surges within me, knowing how fast and powerfully I'm swimming, as comfortable in water as I always feel when I'm surrounded by it, but time rolls by as we take a few turns and the floor drops away slightly without any sign of it ending. Just as I feel hope slipping from my grasp I swim over the sphere that Keneth said he dropped last time he was down here and even though my chest feels tight as my body longs for breath, I know I can hold on longer, I can feel that I have more in me and it spikes my optimism once more and I push myself harder.

As minutes tick by, Keneth slowly pulls away from me, clearly a stronger swimmer than myself and my lungs begin to scream and burn in pain, desperate to inhale, desperate to take in air. My mind starts to feel foggy and I squeeze my mouth as tight as I can, forcing it to stay closed, to let me keep going.

The rope tied to my wrist has slipped off at some point and I must have slowed down quite a bit because Anton's hand pushes at my hip to go forward, his body now almost next to mine. I look at him and grab at my throat, fear coursing through me, because I know that my body is close to giving up the fight. I start to panic and can't swim forward anymore, I flail and shake my head, desperation to survive riding me hard and my mouth opens releasing air that I'd trapped in my lungs. Bubbles of oxygen escape and bubble away from me as Anton swims forward hard, one hand now gripping my forearm in his tight unyielding grasp, dragging me along with him through the tunnel of water.

Losing my mind I flail harder with my eyes clenched closed, it's over. *I can't do this anymore.* Just as I feel my body succumbing and going to breathe the water in, Anton's mouth smashes against mine and he pushes his own air into me and I consume it ravenously.

Opening my eyes in relief, I take a moment to look into his and he pulls me forward to keep swimming. Refusing to waste this temporary opportunity I feel the ground underneath me and push as hard as I can off a rock, swooshing up to Anton's speed and putting every bit of effort into my swimming technique that I can, my mind muddled, tiredness in my core but I refuse to stop again.

Anton suddenly slips behind me and he drops the sphere. I turn my head as I continue swimming to see the light reflecting the horrific scene of Anton wrestling in the water with one of those horrific creatures. *Oh my goodness!* Gremlins can not only swim but they've followed us.

I stop to turn back but Anton furiously waves me away, pointing to his throat, pleading in his eyes. Making it very clear that he doesn't want me to stop in case I run out of air. I frown with my arm out and he shakes his head at me, waving me off again before continuing with his underwater battle.

When I swim away I know that, one of the hardest moments of my entire life was turning around and leaving him there. It is a moment that will live inside me for as long as I live, it's the only regret I have ever known and I will never forgive myself for this. The only thought that pushes me forward is that if I stay and don't survive, I'll kill Keneth too.

I swim for what feels like forever, in the dark now because

both men and their lights are far gone from my view, but it's probably more like a minute or so. My hope is now dead and gone, pure instinct and will to survive are the only things that push me forward, my lungs hurt so badly that I can't bear it and my brain is so light-headed that I'm not sure if I'm swimming or flying anymore. A kind of euphoria takes over me as I glide along in a dream-like state, and for a fleeting moment, I forget why I'm not supposed to breathe.

Dazed and confused I stop swimming and let myself float, my back hits something hard and smooth, *maybe it's the roof.* I look around and wonder what that strange light is that's chasing me, like a funny little firefly swimming up to me. *Maybe I'm dreaming and I could breathe all along? Maybe I'm a firefly?*

I close my eyes when the light gets too bright and decide it's time to breathe and push out all of my air in a big bubbly exhale, and the bubbles tickle my face.

I'm yanked hard and a mouth is slammed against mine. At first, I try to push it away but I'm not strong enough and my lips part at the force and air is forced inside me, and I vaguely remember that I have to hold it in. I open my eyes wearily and see Chuckles staring at me, I wave and smile at him but he frowns at me, grabbing my arm and pulling me along with him. I kick my feet to help him and let him guide me along, but I'm still so tired.

Another dim light floats through the water just ahead and as we approach it I get shoved violently forward by something grabbing my bum and I get propelled through the surface of water and splash down into more water after a short fall. I push my head out of it and take in a deep penetrating breath of air, and it fills me almost painfully as I gasp over and over again, while trying to shake off dizziness that threatens to pull me back under and a current that seems to be sweeping me away.

I reach out and grasp for something to grab, anything. Feeling around, I see a thick branch and swim for it, just making it in time to dig my fingers in and pull myself half on to.

Overwhelmed and slightly nauseous from being underwater too long, I close my eyes and lay with my body on it, just breathing and coming to terms with what just happened.

Anton! All at once I remember what happened and I lift my head up and look back to where I was washed from. About sixty feet back on a ledge with a flow of water flowing over is a sight that makes my heart stop, Keneth and Anton are both on it, intact and alive. However, so is a Gremlin that's trying to get out of the water we must have washed from, Anton is hitting it back down with a large stick as Keneth picks up large rocks and throws it inside the small opening.

"Block the hole!" I scream over to them. "Get bigger rocks and block it so they can't get out."

They turn as I yell over to them and nod at each other in unison as Keneth picks up the biggest boulders he can find while Anton tries to push it back in over and over again.

Anton drops the stick and transforms before my eyes into the Grizzly Bear that he is and starts to pummel his big paws into the rock above, smashing them and showering them down onto the beast below. Keneth copies him and between the two of them they smash the rocks so thoroughly above them that the Gremlin disappears and water fills with heavy stones.

As I watched them, I didn't realise that the branch I'm leaning on has been slowly breaking, snapping little by little, not until it's too late. *Snap!* It cracks in half under my added weight and I drift back down the water at an alarming speed, the sound of roaring water filling my ears and prompting me to see where it's coming from.

"Oh dear Lord." I whisper to myself as I see the water before me disappear over the horizon and I turn just in time to scream, arm outstretched in terror, as both males turn in my direction, eyes wide with shock written all over their features before my body gets sucked forcefully over the edge.

Tumbling down in the air, as liquid pelts me hard from all around, all I can focus on is the watery depths below racing toward me unmercilessly, and in mere seconds I smash hard into it like concrete, pain the last thing I remember before everything's gone.

CHAPTER TWENTY-THREE

Keneth

My whole world stops turning.

Frozen in time, I watch in absolute horror as Janice gets swept over the edge of the waterfall, her eyes wide with fear and hand stretched towards me to save her, to help her, to do... anything. All I could do was watch and die a little bit inside. I will never forget her face before she dropped from my view.

Breathing air back in swiftly after holding it for what seems like years, I dive into the water with zero hesitation and total focus on retrieving my female. My body tenses and stretches as I continue to push myself to the edge, I triple in size and feel the satisfying strength fill me as I roar into the sky at the edge of the drop, bracing for my descent. It'll hurt bad and I couldn't give a damn.

Anton's big body nudges against mine, in the same formidable form that we are both proud of, and we jump together. No thought of self-preservation lingering, just the deep desire to find and save Janice.

The fall is fast and swift, the contact of the water beneath us a heavy sting but nothing more. We are Grizzly's and this is nothing compared to our strength but Janice is a small delicate flower of a female; fragile, soft, and breakable.

Water abruptly surrounds me, and my heavy weight ploughs me to the depth of inky blue water but I will not let nature slow me down. Pushing my legs off the hard, solid floor I use all of my might to blast my way back beyond the surface trying to contain me.

As I break through, my eyes fly open and I scan my surroundings feverishly, seeing nothing in that instant and my heart rate picks up and I let out a growl that sounds more like a howl, swishing my big body back and forth, reaching and flicking my eyes over every surface. *Where is she?*

To my right Anton changes back into his man form, his face furrowed in worry, and eyes squinting in fear. "I'll check the edges." He blurts out with an edge of panic, "You swim deeper in the middle, she has to be here." Turning to shore, Anton swims fast and steady in pursuit of her body.

She has to be alive. I tell myself over and over again as I duck in and under the water, foraging its depths. Despair quickly begins to close in as my search seems more and more in vain. My heartbeat becomes erratic in my chest and I have to stop to catch my breath, pain begins to tear through me, my very heart cracking inside me. The fissures are so clear that I can hear the cracks and tears from inside my mind.

A heart-wrenching bellow fills the air and I turn in the water to find Anton dragging Janice's still form out of the water, his body visibly shaking as he lands with a thump on his knees by her side.

I tear out of the water, transforming into a man as I go, ignoring the gnashing pain ripping through me. Bending over on all fours in the shallows I reach for Janice's delicate foot, touching the soft skin there with the reverence that I feel for every part of her.

"Honey bee," I whisper to her, rising over her barely covered body because Anton's wet shirt has ridden up on her, until my legs straddle hers, resting none of my impressive weight on her. "Please be okay, please." My voice pleading with her, even as she lays lifeless under me, her chest void of any movement.

A whimper sounds next to me and I turn my head slowly to see Anton sitting on his heels, hunched over with his head in his hands, shoulders softly trembling through his silent tears, and I decide then and there that I'm not accepting this.

Leaning over I lift Janice's chin and place my beefy hands on her dainty chest, right over her hands and I start to compress, while watching my strength so that I don't break her. The shifters who worked at Threshold were taught how to care for a female should she stop breathing, and I remember what to do. It was called CPR, and I hope to the Celestials that this works.

"Anton, pray." I speak, continuing my rhythmic compressions on Janice's chest. "I don't care who to. They want these women in the game to help procreate, so maybe they'll listen today."

His head snaps up and looks at me with tear stained cheeks, at first like he's going to fight me on it but his eyes soften when he looks back down to Janice. Nodding once, his head turns back towards the sky, eyelids closed, as he prays for help from one of the many puppeteers who rule us.

While we were in Anton's den, he and I had time to get to

know each other a little better and I know for a fact what he thinks of Guardians and Celestials, and it's certainly not pleasant thoughts. For him to be praying without argument, shows his commitment to *our* Kindred.

I don't know why he fights the truth, it's obvious that she is his, but he refuses to admit it. Even my Bear spirit knows, which is why I never have any jealousy for what they share, it's natural and beautiful. *Why is she not enough for him?*

My heart aches as I pump and pump and pump, never breaking rhythm. Mine and Anton's terror is an almost tangible force in the surrounding air, and I start to find it increasingly hard to keep up my compressions when the pain in my chest intensifies and I begin to feel lightheaded, spots enter my vision and my breathing becomes laboured by my slowing heart rate.

I can't stop. I can't stop. I can't stop. It becomes the mantra that keeps me going, my eyelids now squeezed tightly closed to focus on my control.

"Come on, sweets," I hear through the darkness threatening to take me. "We need you, come back to us."

Opening my tired eyes, I try my hardest to refocus my efforts, swaying slightly as I do, and Anton strokes Janice's hair softly off her ashen face.

Suddenly unable to breath, pain strikes me hard in the centre of my heart and I collapse on my side, body tumbling off Janice in a last bid to not crush her. My body is done and I can't fight anymore, the thumping in my chest now slow and heavy, fighting until the very end, refusing to shatter.

Struggling to keep my eyes open now, I slowly reach out and weakly grasp a hold of Janice's slender fingers, wishing that I could have saved her. Wishing a lot of things.

Anton rises over her body, with a quick glance down at me,

and an angry look takes over his features, they harden all over, from the thin line of his mouth to the steel in his eyes.

"Nooo!" Anton yells out, his hands clasp together above his head. "I said nooo!" His clapped fists drop hard on Janice's chest and I hear a crack, probably a rib breaking.

CHAPTER TWENTY-FOUR

Floating amongst a sea of peace, euphoric tides lapping upon my skin, I have never known a more content feeling of home before. A soft internal embrace lulls me, stripping me of all the pain I've ever known and leaves me, strangely whole.

"Child," a whimsical voice reverberates the space around me, rippling through my existence, "I have come to speak with you. Stand and open your eyes, my sweet child."

I'm not sure how, but I became aware of my feet on a smooth, warm surface and my eyes that I forgot I had, open.

Taking a moment to figure out where I am, I notice the inky liquid of the world around me, rippling constantly with every movement and blink I make, like shiny satin shimmering in the light that doesn't come from anywhere that I can see and the velvety depth beyond swallows the world that isn't. I don't feel confused. I don't feel scared. I just am.

From the depths of darkness, a figure emerges, gliding through with ease and eerie beauty. The figure is a woman, if you can call her that for the title is not enough for whom I see now before me, a tall, glorious, dark beauty with a sizable glimmering sickle, wild long hair as white as snow billowing around her as if she were swimming, her pale ice eyes piercing into my soul so accurately that I feel her searching beneath my skin, and it comforts me.

"That's it, my child, do not fear me for I am here on request. I have been in the prayers of those who wish you life, those who beg for your return." Her gaze holds me still and reverent. "Tell me my dear, do you seek restoration?"

I move my tongue inside my mouth to see if it works and then lick my lips before replying, "Who are you?" My voice is no more than a whisper.

She quirks her head to the side, eyes briefly glittering with humour before they steady once more, "I am the Goddess Azraelle, the bringer of life, death, and rebirth. Answer my question child, for your time is running out."

I think about Keneth and how he will die when I do, and about Anton being left behind, living in his guilt and self-loathing, all alone and it's clear to me that I have to go back. For them if not for me.

"Ye..." I pause, remembering all that I have learned about the Celestials recently. "What's the price?" I reword before I agree, feeling as though this was, perhaps, too easy.

The rippling around me intensifies until the world vibrates around us, and for the first time since being here, I feel fear trickle down my spine.

Goddess Azraelle's shoulders tense and she clenches her sickle harder. Breathing in deeply she replies, "You're not a silly human, are you?" Her voice is no longer melodic but harsh and echoing in the space. "While you have offended me by challenging my offer, I see no reason to lie to you."

She looks away into the darkness, her mouth set in a somber downturn, "Soon will come a time when I will call for you, your

Kindred, and any future spawn." Turning back to me, her voice now with a tinge of sadness she says, "Your price is that you shall come to me when I summon you and you *will* fight in my honour. It may be in a year or a thousand years, but you will come."

"I don't know how to fight. You're a Goddess, what could I possibly do that you can't?" I shake my head in confusion.

With a small smile lacing her lips, Goddess Azraelle starts to fade away in front of me, "You're out of time child. Choose." I step forward and she is almost fully gone, her voice no more than a distant echo in the darkness, "Choose..."

"Take me back." I cry out desperately, thinking I'm too late. "Please, I'll do whatever you want."

The inky liquid around me lifts high above me, tightening its grip around me until I am compressed and staring up at the wave forming above all around me. It crashes down on me with a heavy weight, thrusting down my screaming throat and drowning me in seconds.

* * *

A LOUD CRACK and a violent pain in my chest wrenches me back into reality, my lungs and throat burn as I turn my head to the side and start to vomit water, coughing continuously trying to remember how to breathe.

I get pushed over to my side and something whacks my back over and over again as I continue to hack up my lungs, or at least that's what it feels like. I cling desperately to my chest and throat, craving air and relief from the pain.

Finally able to breathe again without any more water coming up, I'm suddenly grabbed around my waist to get hoisted up and I shout out in pain as it slices through my chest and shoulder. That small movement was enough to make me very aware of how much pain I'm really in.

"Fuck." I hear the familiar voice of Anton say, "I think I broke something."

Laying back down, I carefully roll onto my back, one hand on my chest and the other on my shoulder.

Keneth's face appears above me with tears freely streaming down his cheeks, "Honey bee, I thought I lost you." His big hand moves my smaller one from my shoulder and I wince. "You must have dislocated your shoulder in the fall, I'm going to put it back in okay?" His sweet eyes look into mine for reassurance.

I nod once and turn my head away ready for the pain. I've dislocated my shoulder once before, and it's not the kind of pain that you forget. I know it'll be a brief pain, but I also know it'll suck, big time. "Do it." I croak out.

Keneth takes a deep breath, his face contorted like he doesn't want to do it either and then grabs my arm in the right position. "Just breathe. One... Two..." He pops it back in before he gets to three and I scream, my chest hurts even more when I do.

Anton strokes my hair cooing, "It's alright, it's over now. You're gonna be okay." I look up at him with shallow pants from my sore chest and he seems gentler than I remember.

"What happened?" I ask them, looking from one to the other. I'm a little bit confused as to why I'm lying here with my body so sore. I vaguely remember a waterfall and... a lady...

Oh my Goddess!

Before they can answer I jolt to an upright position, wincing with my hand to my chest. "The Goddess!" I cry out, looking around frantically.

"What Goddess, honey bee?" Keneth asks with a confused frown, and Anton stiffens beside me, suddenly white as a ghost.

"Goddess Azraelle, where is she?" All of my memories come

flooding back to me with a whoosh. "It worked. It actually worked."

Keneth puts his big hand on my good shoulder and squeezes reassuringly, "I think you might have had a dream. You're not making any sense."

I search his gaze pleadingly and then turn to Anton who is still stock still. *He knows something.* "Anton?" I question him, eyes wide.

"I can't believe they actually listened." He states, as he looks me up and down as if he's assessing me for some other unknown injury. "I tried any that I thought might have the best chance of helping, but I never thought Goddess Azraelle would be the one to answer. Did she talk to you?"

Keneth blurts out, "Holy crap! You talked to one of the Gods? Awesome, I can't freaking believe it worked." Keneth's enthusiasm is clear as he put his fist out for Anton to fist-bump, but he just solemnly looked at it before turning back to me for my answer. Keneth deflated a little bit after being left hanging.

"I'm sorry, I had to make a deal but I couldn't just let you die, Chuckles." My impromptu actions weighed on me and all I can hope for is that he'll forgive me. I grab his hand and squeeze.

Keneth tilts his head to the side and frowns, "I don't care what you had to do as long as you're back here with me."

"What did you agree to?" Anton blurts out, concern in his voice.

I smack my lips together and swallow hard, my throat feels like I ate razor blades. Finding my voice I speak, "I promised that we would fight for her one day if she asked. Me, my Kindred, and my *spawn*, as she put it." I scowl at that untasteful term for children.

Keneth smiles broadly and it lights him up, all the way to his eyes. "That's great, honey bee, the Celestials never have reason to fight, so it'll never be an issue. Thank the Goddess for her blessing of life."

Anton looks unconvinced.

"I've never heard of her." I admit. The only God I'd ever bothered to learn about was the Lord almighty, the rest was all just fairytales. The whole idea of the Celestials is still so new to me and if I'm being honest with myself, frightening.

Keneth gently lifts me up like I weigh nothing and places me in his lap. "She's a Celtic Deity, not very widely known honestly, but her power is nothing to sneeze at. As I'm sure you've figured out by now." He nuzzles my cheek lovingly and proceeds to kiss me all over my face. "How are you feeling? Be honest."

I lean into him and relax, letting my body mould into his until I feel safe and protected again. "I'm alive." I try to deeply sigh but the pain in my chest prevents me and a moan escapes instead. "I'm also darn sore, what happened to my chest? I feel like I was hit with a truck." I smile tightly, so they don't fret too much.

"CPR love." Keneth says with a small chuckle. "It saved your life, but I'm pretty sure it also broke your rib. Sorry."

I flick my hand dismissively, "Don't be silly, it'll heal. Thank you, both of you." I turn my head and look at the bushy scenery behind us and the water hole and waterfall in front of us. "Where are we? Did we get rid of the creatures?"

"Sure did, sweets. They're long gone." Anton speaks up. "They won't be coming out where we did, but to be sure that they aren't nearby, we should get moving as soon as you're able to. Last thing we need is another ambush."

Reaching over, I grab his hand, remembering that I thought he'd died in the water tunnel. "How did you make it out? I was sure you were a goner, leaving you there was the hardest thing I've ever had to do. It broke my heart, I'm so sorry." I let go of his hand

and stroke his cheek and he leans toward me so that it's easier for me.

We stare into each other's eyes for a few minutes before Keneth clears his throat. "Sorry to break up, whatever that is, but I think it's time we go and find some safe shelter for the night. The sun is starting to drop and I don't know about you guys, but I'm exhausted. I'm talking physically, mentally, and emotionally drained."

Nodding in agreement with Keneth, the guys stand up and help me to my feet slowly, my chest still throbbing in pain.

I pull my saturated oversized shirt down to give myself some form of modesty, when Keneth lifts me up like a bride, careful to keep the shirt over my bottom as he does it.

"Son of a gun, Mr Chuckles, you make me feel as light as a feather," I giggle out. "A cold, wet feather granted, but still a feather."

Anton comes behind me and wrings out my ashy blond hair. "When we find a safe place we'll hang the clothes up to dry and keep you warm, little feather. Don't you worry about that." I blush as he pats me softly on the behind and then walks in front of us, taking the lead on the next part of our little adventure.

CHAPTER TWENTY-FIVE

The proverbial road feels long and tiring as we trek our way back toward civilization again. The warm sun slowly drying out our wet clothes and hair as we plod along together in companionable silence, a silence that I could never imagine myself immersing in.

I've always felt the need to surround myself in sound, whether it be by talking, humming, or a loud atmosphere, but as I take this journey hand in hand with my Kindred and this unpredictable man that I have no suitable label for, because friend just doesn't quite cut it, I find that the peace of their company is all I've ever needed. It's like they complete the piece of me that I never knew was missing until I had them by my side.

I don't know what will become of us and I'm not afraid to find out, because somehow I just know that it'll be okay.

"Where is your mind at, honey bee?" Keneth breaks me out of my reverie. "You look a million miles away." He squeezes my hand tight and pulls me under his arm, wrapping me in his woodsy scent.

Sighing deeply in satisfaction I gaze up at him. "I am." My smile grows bright at his confused expression. "'I'm thinking about a future that I can't even begin to understand, and how lucky I am to have you both in my life."

Anton pretends to dry heave. "Ew. Don't be sentimental and weird or I'm taking you back to the Gremlins."

I swat at his arm playfully with the back of my hand and he snickers at me in jest. "Oh, shush you. You can't fool me, Mister, I know you're a softy on the inside."

The trees begin to part as we come across a small tudor village, a few people bustling about on the makeshift road between the buildings.

"This'll do for the night." Anton says walking forward toward a stoutly looking gentleman hoeing at a garden bed. "Excuse me, Sir, do you know of a place we might be able to sleep for the evening?"

I screw up my face at his change of tone and body language. Watching his bright friendly smile and open hands in polite greeting. *Who is this person and what has he done with the Grizzly I know?*

I hear Keneth chuckle next to me, covering his mouth to try and hide it.

"What is happening right now? Did he hit his head or something?" I whisper to him in disbelief.

Leaning into my ear he replies softly, "He smells of a Panda shifter. I think Anton's trying to appear non-threatening."

The Panda farmer scowls at Anton for a minute with distrust, clearly about to tell him to get lost when his attention goes to Keneth and I standing behind him. His face instantly changes as he takes me in and with a slight bow toward me the corner of his lips go up in a jovial smile, and instantly I recognise him as an ally.

There's nothing but kindness radiating between the depths of his whiskey coloured eyes.

"Good afternoon, female, are you in any distress?" He asks straight to the point, his gaze flicking over my attire and the two males by me in obvious concern.

I return his smile warmly, appreciating his unnecessary protectiveness. "Hello there," I step towards him happily, pushing away Keneth's hand as he goes to grab for me. "I'm Janice, and I'm perfectly safe, thank you for asking. We've been travelling all day though and as you can see we've lost all of our luggage. Is there anywhere that we may rest for the night?"

He nods once, his eyes glittering with happiness. "Of course, of course. Please follow me." He places his hoe on the wall, wiping his dirty hands down his overalls and gestures for us to follow him. "You wouldn't be hungry by any chance? My brother is making a big pot of vegetable stew, and we would be delighted if you would join us."

"No." Anton says at the same time that I say, "Yes, thank you."

I look at him with a frown. "You can go without if you like but..." I turn to our hospitable friend, "I, for one, would be honoured."

Anton grumbles out a resultant acceptance and Keneth laughs quietly, joining my side and speaking low, says, "So much for his politeness." Raising his voice again he acknowledges the man in front of us with a friendly demeanour. "Thank you kindly, friend. My Kindred is in need of food and rest, and I will have to owe you for your hospitality this evening. I have no way to repay you until later I'm afraid as we only have the clothes on our back." I can't help but notice Keneth's proud stance as he claims me as his mate to this stranger and it warms my heart.

"Nonsense." He replies jovially, waving his hand in the air, "It is our pleasure to help, and of course we will supply you all with a fresh pair of clothes and a warm place to sleep." He turns and looks me up and down with a frown. "I'm not sure if we will have anything your size, Janice, but I'll see what I can come up with."

Anton growls low in his throat, "Be very careful how you look at her, Panda!" The words come out maliciously and I slap his back.

"Mind your manners, Anton! He is our host and he was looking at me with no disrespect and you know it." I put my hands on my hips and scowl up at him. "Either leave your Grizzly attitude outside or you can stay out here and sit with the carrots!"

With a huff, he reluctantly nods in agreement to behave.

The Panda man clears his throat in an attempt to hide his shock and amusement of how I spoke to Anton. "It's quite alright and understandable. Kindreds are meant to be possessive of their females, I'm sure you'd feel the same way if it was the other way around. Now please, let's go inside, dinner should be ready by now."

Ambling ahead of us we follow him inside the first house on the left. It is a cute old Tudor home, clearly lived in and loved by the owners, and just like every other house I've seen since arriving, missing a feminine touch.

The furniture is plain and dark with no decorative adornments throughout the living spaces inside or out. It feels homely and the aromatic scent of stew wafts throughout the small space, making my mouth water and my stomach growl in protest.

When we sit down in the living room a taller and older version of the Panda man sitting across from us enters the room from a side door.

He stops in shock as he takes the three of us in, his dark eyes lingering on me for longer than comfortable. "James, is there a female in here or have I finally lost my mind?" He asks in astonishment, eyes still latched on my own.

"Jeez, Daniel, is it absolutely necessary that you stare at her?" The Panda man, apparently named James says in horror, as he stands in front of his brother, breaking our connection. "Her Kindreds are going to let loose any minute."

I look to the right of me and see both Anton and surprisingly, Keneth, sitting at the edge of their seat, teeth bared in threat.

Blinking rapidly, Daniel looks at the men and takes a retreating step back before dropping his gaze to the floor in submission. "I apologise, I've just never seen a female other than our Maman." His tone is regretful and sad.

I stand up, feeling instantly sorry for him. "It's okay, don't worry about it. I'm Janice." I wave coyly and smile, the reminder of how desolate the men in Rathe must be a heavy weight on my heart. "I hope you don't mind, but your brother invited us to try the delicious smelling stew you're making."

With the reminder my tummy growls again on cue, making Keneth chuckle behind me, breaking any tension remaining in the room.

Daniel beams a smile at me and bows at the waist like I'm royalty or something. "Yes, please. I can't guarantee that it's as good as you're making it sound though."

"Oh my gosh, are you kidding? I haven't been fed a real meal in what feels like weeks, it will be absolute heaven to me." I rub my belly in anticipation, unable to keep the smile off my lips.

I notice both Daniel and James gaze behind me in confusion at the men at my back, before they cover it quickly and show us to a bedroom down a long hallway. Just like the rest of the house the room is basic and practical.

I use their facilities, and when I return to the bedroom, I find

James inside giving clothes to the men for us to change into before dinner.

Both Anton and Keneth manage to get shirts and shorts that fit well enough but all there is for me to wear is an oversized shirt and giant denim overalls that they cut into shorts for me. I look ridiculous and I love it.

* * *

Sitting down for dinner we fall into comfortable discussion as our hosts tell us about their simple farm and their love for the country life. They are both really sweet guys and I find myself thoroughly enjoying their conversation.

I tell them all about my life back on Earth and watch their fascination over how many women there are and how many children are just running all over the place and it really brings to the fore how lucky I was to have my life into focus. It hurts me to think of a whole world filled with loneliness and the deep desire for love and companionship, while on Earth, so many people take their partners and children for granted.

One day I pray for this world to fill with the laughter and joy that only children can bring. A day when our world's truly collide.

I have a staggering three bowls of stew before my stomach is so full that I might just pop. I groan in a mixture of satisfaction and discomfort as I slide down my chair, eyes closed and hand rubbing my now extended tummy.

"Goodness gracious, I ate way too much." I half whimper.

The whole table laughs boisterously in agreement.

"I honestly don't know where you put it all." Daniel chuffs out in amusement.

"Me neither." I admit with another groan.

Keneth leans down and rubs my belly slowly in circles, trying to relieve some of my discomfort. "Come on, honey bee, we should go to bed so you can stretch out. Plus we still have a few hours of walking to do in the morning. We'll need to leave with the sun if we're going to get there on time." He kisses me tenderly on my temple and I nod because he's totally right.

"So where are you three off to in the morrow anyway?" James asked as he clears our plates away.

The answering silence has me opening my eyes and looking around. Both Keneth and Anton are avoiding their gaze and I realise that they don't know what to say.

"To the market." I put in, disturbing the quiet growing in the room. "We're going to fix some wrongs."

James almost drops the plates he's holding and Daniel sucks in a hard breath. Clearly they know what market I'm talking about for it to have that response.

"You can't go there!" Daniel stuns me by shouting out and my gaze flicks to him at his sudden outburst. Daniel had been very soft-spoken and pleasant all evening and his sudden raise in voice more than shocked me.

"Daniel!" James tries to shush his brother.

Daniel looks around at him and then back at us, "But she'll be taken." Is all he can say, fear evident in his features.

"We have it all under control, no need to worry." Anton tries to placate him, but his voice is weaker than usual. The guilt I know that he feels, weighing down the conviction that he normally puts into his words.

I tap the table softly with a smile, deciding to change the subject. "Thank you for such a lovely meal, but I'm afraid that if I don't lay down I might just burst." I stand and the men follow my actions instantly, still on edge. "Would you like some help with the dishes?" I ask.

Snapping out of his weird mood Daniel replies, "Not at all, I cook and James cleans. He's not getting out of that so easily."

James pretends to huff off but turns back with a quick wink to me as he calls out, "Such a bully, my big brother." Then disappears into the kitchen.

Taking that as the perfect time to disentangle ourselves from the situation, we say our goodnights and retire to the bedroom provided to us.

Entering the room and closing the door behind us, we pause to take in the Queen sized bed before us. *Who says three's a crowd?*

"I'm taking the middle." I say as I undo my overalls and start crawling up the bed.

Tucking myself under the soft blanket in the centre of the bed, I wait patiently as both men just stare down at me with looks of a different kind of hunger.

I giggle and cover myself as both of them run and jump on the bed, mischief dancing in their eyes.

Keneth flips the blankets back at the same time as Anton's starts to relentlessly tickle my ribs. It's amazing how quick my ribs healed from this whole Kindred thing. The only pain I feel is a dull ache now.

"No." I squeal. "Mercy! Mercy!"

Keneth dives down to my flailing feet and torments me even more and I laugh so hard that I can't breathe, lungs aching for air from the assault.

Before I realise what's happening, Keneth climbs up between my legs nipping and licking up the inside of my thighs, and they part of their own will as I groan at his sensitive touches. Anton's hands slip from my ribs, up and over my pebbling breasts, tweaking my nipples through the fabric and looking down at me with a growing lust.

With hooded eyes, Anton slowly lowers his mouth to mine,

softly taking my bottom lip between his teeth and pulling at the same time that Keneth reaches my sex, his tongue lightly tasting my wet lips. The double sensation making me arch my back and moan.

"I love the taste of your honey." Keneth says, vibrating the words along my pulsing nub.

I don't know how this got so dirty so fast, but I'm not complaining one bit.

"I wish I could stick my hard cock deep into that soaking wet pussy." Anton all but growls as he kisses along the line of my jaw. "I bet it feels fucking amazing."

Leaning up, I bite his neck gently and whisper into his ear as I lick his lobe. "Fuck me then. I want to feel you gliding inside me."

I feel him shudder under my words and Keneth pushes a finger inside me and then starts to suck on my clit.

I reach down to pull his hair and grind myself against his face, panting and mewling for more.

Looking up at Anton I see that he's pulled away, with a look of a man possessed. "I can't." He breathes out, regret filling his eyes. "I'm sorry, I just can't." And with that he gets up and stalks out of the room, slamming the door behind him.

I suck in a hard breath, shocked by his swift change in behaviour.

Keneth crawls up to me and kisses me tenderly, the sweet taste of me still on his lips. "He's determined to hurt himself, don't let it ruin the mood, love."

Wrapping my arms around his neck I stare up at him, confused. "I don't understand, it's not like he hasn't been inside me before."

"That was from behind, honey bee, it's different." He strokes my cheek, and continues explaining. "We have been without females for a long time, you need to understand anal isn't a big thing for us here because that's all we know, but to be truly inside a female, to fill her womb with seed, that is what it takes to claim a Kindred. I thought you understood that?"

With awe, I look into his face and recognise the honesty written on his features. "No, we weren't told that." Is all I say, because my mind is reeling, by not only how a claiming is truly done, but also with the obvious knowledge that with a world of only men, sexual fluidity would be normal. I can't believe I've never realised this before.

Keneth frowns down at me. "What's wrong? Did I say something bad?"

I shake my head, because nothing *is* wrong, I'm just taken aback but how ignorant I was in not realising it sooner.

"Did you sleep with many men?" I ask, unable to help my curiosity.

He stiffens above me before answering. "I don't know what you want me to say." Keneth rolls off me and lies on his back with his hand over his eyes, hiding from me.

"Please don't block yourself from me. I don't care, I was just curious, that's all." I try to reassure him, pulling his arm down and snuggling into him.

He sighs, "I'm not ashamed. There are quite a few males who enjoy it but for me, it was always a means to an end and something I have only done twice because I really couldn't get into it. It's just not my thing."

Deciding that the mood has well and truly passed, I stroke his chest softly and settle against him even more. "I love you, silly, and I couldn't care less." I say in all honesty, because I truly don't care.

All that matters is that I am his and he is mine, but it certainly makes more sense now why Anton won't have sex with me in that way. I never wanted to push him, I hope he comes back to bed soon.

I fall asleep with Keneth whispering sweet nothings in my ear, and no Anton in sight.

CHAPTER TWENTY-SIX

The unmistakable fragrance of fresh tea hits my nose and fills my mouth with water before I even manage to open my eyes to the new day ahead.

With a gleeful, animated squish of my face, I squint up at the delicious shirtless male specimen before me, holding a fresh cup of tea and jestful eyes at my obvious delight.

"Good morning, Kindred, I thought you might appreciate a cup of tea since I've heard you moan about missing it in our recent mornings together." My sweet Keneth says, as my heart flutters from his romantic gesture, and it is romantic. There's nothing quite as special as when the person you love brings you the right type of caffeine first thing in the morning.

I sit up in the bed and wrap my arms around his taut waist, giving him an affectionate squeeze and a quick peck in the centre of his impressive abs. "Thank you, my love." Sitting back against the headboard, he gives me my tea carefully so as not to spill it and lowers his massive body to the side of my bed, easing himself against me.

"You looked like you might sleep the day away." He starts and my brain quickly registers that we were meant to leave at sun up and it's clearly been up for a while by the light filtering through the window. Putting his hands up to stop my pending panic at sleeping in, he continues, "Don't stress, the market will go all day and it's only a couple of hours away. You can ride me if you're really worried about it."

"Ride you, hey?" I joke with a wink, deciding not to stress about something that I have no control of.

With his signature chuckle, Keneth strokes the side of my face lovingly before I take a sip of what has to be a piece of heaven.

As the sweet taste caresses my tongue and the warm liquid slides down my throat, I moan with pure satisfaction. The moment it touched my eager lips, I was lost in the moment, thoroughly under its ambrosian spell.

"Should we leave you alone with that?" I hear a gruff voice say from the doorway and I pop my eyes open to peer over at Anton, leaning on the door frame to the bedroom.

"I didn't hear you come back in." I say, my voice small, even to my own ears.

He huffs out a breath and takes a couple of steps into the room. "I slept on the couch last night. Figured that I should give you two some space." His hands are deep in his pockets and he kicks at an imaginary object on the floor, looking slightly uncomfortable and unsure for the first time ever.

Keneth pops up from the bed and looks down at me. "I'm to go and see if the Panda brothers need a hand with anything before we head off." Keneth politely excuses himself from the oncoming conversation, walking out with a quick nod in greeting to Anton.

After taking another quick sip of my tea, I put it on the dresser next to me before pulling the blankets off and placing my feet on the smooth wooden slatted floor.

"Sit with me." I pat the bed beside me but he just looks down at my exposed legs, taking them in, inch by inch until flicking his eyes back to my gaze. "Come on, I won't bite... unless you want me too." Adding the last bit to lighten the mood.

Anton's eyes darken and become hooded, and I realise that I may have said the wrong thing. His heavy gait feels predatory as he approaches me, never taking his eyes off my own, he pushes his legs between mine, making my thighs open wide to accommodate his large frame.

With my shirt riding up, my core becomes totally exposed and with his gaze burning into me, he lowers himself onto his knees before making my heart thud loud and hard in my chest, my breath picking up into a more shallow pant.

Slowly placing his rough, calloused hands on my slender knees, he pushes them apart even further and slowly drops his molten gaze onto my now weeping core. *Fuck.*

I place my trembling hands on his freshly shaved head and glide them over the soft, warm surface, needing to just touch him while feeling so vulnerable and exposed.

A deep rumble rises from his throat at my touch. "I'll miss the way your pussy drips for me, sweets." His ungodly baritone voice says in the most seductive tone, making *said* pussy clench with a need that will never be filled.

Clearing my throat I rasp out, "Why are you doing this?" Needing to know why he'd torture me like this, when it's obvious that I want him, even if he doesn't want me in the same way.

Closing his chestnut eyes he leans forward and rests his head on my chest, which I'm sure is pounding with the heavy beats of my heart. "I don't know." His voice is so low that I almost didn't hear it.

I pull his head up to look at me and am shocked by what I see;

guilt, desperation, and despair. "Anton, what's wrong?" I smooth my thumb along the furrowed lines in his forehead. "Talk to me."

"I'm sorry that you have to go to this stupid fucking market for me but I'm not sorry I kidnapped you." I'm taken aback by his words, not quite sure how I should take them. "I'm not sorry that we were trapped, or that I was injured, and sure as fuck not sorry that I met you." He continues, and I squint in confusion.

"Janice, you've changed my life in the worst and best way, and I don't know how to deal with that. I'm an asshole, I know, and I'm not about to change anytime soon, but somehow you still find it in you to look at me the way you are now and I don't deserve it." He slides his hands up the outside of my thighs until he grabs my hips, pulling me further into him. "I want you to know that even though I can't give you what you want, I am grateful to know you and my biggest apology is that you can't be mine, but I know in the future you'll be glad that you weren't stuck with a wretch like me for a Kindred. Keneth will make you happy and be a good breeder for you, but I hope that you find another mate one day, one that's just as deserving as he is because I want you to live a long life, for you and for any future cubs you might have."

Leaning up to give me a soft kiss to my slightly parted lips, he lingers there while we breathe in each other's air, bathing in the moment of unity between us before he whispers on my lips, "Thank you." And then stands up and leaves the room, and me still sitting on the edge of the bed, legs parted, and a heart hurting from what will never be.

* * *

AFTER PUTTING my heart back together and a quick breakfast with Daniel and James, we say our goodbyes and give our gratitude to our most hospitable hosts, feeling appreciative of our new-found friends.

Heading down a somewhat overgrown path, we walk in silence. This time, a rather awkward one; Anton tense and uncomfortable with his honesty from earlier, me overwhelmed by what was said and what's to come, and poor Keneth unaware and unsure of what happened to make everything so tense in the first place but too polite and sweet to ask.

An hour passes before Keneth decides to fill it with conversation fillers, and not before long the three of us are chatting away about nothing important but great for a more light-hearted walk.

I find out that Chuckles is one of four boys, having grown up in a mixed pack of Grizzlies, Wolves and Coyotes on the other side of the country where his family still resides. When he turned eighty, he decided on a change of pace and travelled for a while before finding a new pack to call his own, majoritively Grizzly but sharing the same woods as Summer's Kindred's pack.

I'd heard of them before and was surprised that I hadn't remembered him from when I was back there, especially the night of the twins' birth. I assumed every shifter in the area had shown up, with the large mix in the territory at the time.

Anton however had been a rogue Bear until getting mixed up with the six-pack. The stupid name still making me laugh wholeheartedly.

It's kind of strange to think how far the three of us have come together in such a short period of time, even though it feels like it's been forever since Summer's babies were born. I often wonder how they're doing, I hope she's not too stressed about my disappearance.

I also think a lot about Havana and the girls, while I know that Nateesha and Alice got away, I have no idea what became of poor

Havana. She's such a delicate flower of a girl and I hate the idea that she's out there somewhere scared and alone with a possible deviant.

Anton doesn't really put my mind at ease about it either, certain that his less than stellar friend will be taking her directly to the market and in the hands of more terrible men. At least he isn't lying to me just to make me feel better, I suppose.

The path we trudge down eventually starts to look more like a road and my anxiety picks up a notch, as sweat lines my palm and my breathing increases.

"Tell me the plan." I state, needing to be prepared about what I'm getting myself into, and mentally reminding myself that it's for a good cause.

Keneth grunts unhappily. "Just for the record, I'm still a hundred percent against this." He squeezes my hand tight for effect.

"I know, love, but it's happening so let's be productive instead of negative okay?" I remind him to make it clear that I'm not budging.

Anton rubs his hand along the back of his neck, face dour and tense. "I'm known there, so I will just walk you up to whoever is there and he will probably cuff you and lead you off to one of the cages, and I'll be directed to the Sorcerer in charge of the wishes exchange.

"While we're doing that, Keneth can go off and find his fellow knights in shining armour and let them know what's going on. They should have a representative that'll appeal on his behalf due to you being his claimed Kindred and if all goes well they will release you back in plenty of time for me to get my wish." Anton finishes with a resigned sigh, shoulders rising and falling hard with its intensity.

"And if they don't just hand me over?" I ask, because it's a very real possibility.

Keneth places his heavy arm around my shoulders and pulls me into his side, "Then I will just have to buy you, my honey bee." He kisses the top of my head. "You're worth every gold coin I own, and Threshold gave me *many*."

His reassurance and light words takes the edge off my anxiety a little bit. Even though he's obviously against me doing this, he seems to have full confidence in getting me back, and that helps a lot.

I reach over and tug on Anton's sleeve to get his attention. "Hey." He turns to me without actually meeting my eyes. "What are you going to do after you get your wish?"

Pursing his lips to one side he says, "Get the hell out of there as quickly as I can. I have no idea how well they're going to take me handing in an already claimed female, and I don't intend to hang around long enough to find out, if you get my drift."

I frown, "Your den is ruined. Where will you go?" Worry and guilt fills me at him being homeless and possibly in trouble for what's about to happen.

"Never you worry, sweets. I'm a big boy and can take care of myself. It's not the first time I've been homeless with someone after me and I doubt it'll be the last." He smiles confidently, showing his teeth in mischief.

I shake my head in bewilderment. "You're a worry, you know that?" I scoff at his unapologetic way of life. "Are we going to see you again?" My chest tightens at the question I've been too afraid to ask until now.

With Anton's face sobering, he pulls on his earlobe and answers, "One day I'm sure we'll cross paths again. We live in a big world but it's a long-lived one, and it's almost impossible not to come across the same people eventually." He squeezes in a tight fake smile. "Maybe by then you can meet my Kindred."

Facing the front again Anton picks up his pace and I find myself speechless and snuggling closer under Keneth's warm embrace as we near our final destination in our long journey. The top of the buildings in town come into view as we stroll out of the woods and onto a long green plane, littered with purple and white wild flowers that fill my nose with the sweet scent of freedom. What a beautiful sight for a scary, unpredictable day.

CHAPTER TWENTY-SEVEN

The crazy hustle and bustle of the busy town takes me off guard as I glance around in every direction, overwhelmed by the masses of people in a hurry to scurry off this way and that.

The streets are so busy that people are rubbing up against each other as they walk, not an 'excuse me' to be heard. Of course the only people I see are men though. All shapes and sizes, big and small, wide and thin, dark and light. Not only that but some random animals roam the borders trotting their way to their chosen destinations. It's all a bit like a crazy, messy dream that doesn't quite make sense.

I've never seen so many men all in one place before and even though they are all so different from each other, one thing remains to be true; there's not one ugly duckling among them and every one of them managed to stop and stare at me as we push our way through.

This is a single woman's paradise and I'm surprised by my lack of motivation to perve on any of them, feeling totally satisfied by the two strapping males at my side instead.

Just as I begin to get use to the odd spectacle of this town, I spot a little Latino looking male with eyes the colour of grey stone place his hands over a petite ginger gentleman sitting before him, when his hands lights up a peculiar teal shade, pulsing like bright transparent liquid fire onto the other man's scalp. His curly ginger hair quickly changes to a black crew cut before my eyes, making me gasp loudly in surprise, catching the attention of the obviously magical Latino who gives me a cheeky wink before going back to work.

My head snaps in the chuckling Keneth's direction, "What was that?" I squeal in delight, stunned by what I saw.

"That is a Sorcerer, honey bee. Remember? We talked about that." The lines around his eyes deepen with his enjoyment of my reaction. My mind flicks back to instantly remember that Sorcerers are like some kind of fancy witches or something.

All of a sudden I feel really giddy at the prospect of all the different Mhanu that I might see today, having forgotten all about it in my early nervousness.

I spend the rest of the walk taking in every detail that I can about the men around me, shamelessly staring at them like they do to me. Not for too dissimilar reasons either, I realise, they would be just as fascinated by a female among them as I am with what breed of Mhanu they would be. The only major difference being that I hold no lust in my eyes while theirs are dripping with it.

To my delight, both Anton and Keneth seem to let me ogle every person I pass and vice versa without any unnecessary male posturing on their part.

I managed to spot all sorts of exciting things including more different coloured magic displays, gills on the side of some necks, pointed ears, someone dancing with fire in their hands, glimmering wings of transparent silk, and another Angel.

Then in a shock, I catch sight of three tall, well muscled women stalking through the street, all the male's giving them a wide berth and blatantly looking away from their direction. One has short carrot spiral curls framing a surprisingly delicate face and shoulders, one is a very busty woman with long straight black hair down to her bottom and the last one of Asian orient, slightly smaller than the other two and with shocking fire engine red hair cut short and choppy, like a hair Picasso. All three of them sport tight leather short bodysuits and weapons of different kinds adorn their bodies. Clearly these are the Valkyrie.

Keneth grabs my face and pulls me in for a deep kiss, dragging me under an awning and pushes me against a cold hard wall with his body, delving his hungry tongue into my mouth and making me forget my own name.

I grasp at the ends of his blond mane and ravenously kiss him back, lifting my leg around his hip and pulling him in closer to grind myself against him.

"Fucking hell." I hear Anton curse behind Keneth. "They're gone, you can cut it out now before we get an unwanted audience." He grumbles.

His words catch my attention and I push Keneth away and scowl at him. "Were you distracting me?"

He has the good sense to at least look coy before replying. "It worked didn't it."

I shove him off me in frustration. "Why on Earth would you do that?"

"Not on Earth, sweets, how many times do I have to tell you that?" Anton buttons in.

"Oh, shush it." I snap at him, not looking away from Keneth with my firm scowl and cross my arms over my chest.

Keneth pulls my arms away, eyes apologetic. "I'm sorry, honey bee, but you can't look directly at them or they'll attack you." He apologises. "I didn't want you to get hurt."

I roll my eyes petulantly. "You could have just told me." I grumble out, with a very unladylike snort.

"Now where would be the fun in that?" He asks mischievously, pulling me back in for a quick peck.

"Sorry to break up this sickening display of feelings, but we're gonna have to part ways now so I can hand Janice in." Anton interrupts.

Keneth's face hardens and he slowly turns to face Anton, a low growl building in his throat. "If anything goes wrong I will come for your life, Bear, do you hear me?" The threat is clear and unrepentant. "There will be nowhere you can hide from me if she is taken."

Nodding in complete agreement, Anton says, "If anything happens to this female my life will be forfeit to you without hesitation, my friend. I don't want anything to befall her either."

With a scoff Keneth replies, "You are a foolish male and you will regret ever turning her away, mark my words."

Turning back to me, Keneth's features soften again and I have to blink away sneaky tears that try to fill my eyes without my permission. "I'll be fine, Chuckles." I smile, even though my lips involuntarily tremble. "Get ready to save me again, my love."

Going on my tiptoes I kiss the cute button at the tip of his nose, his left cheek and then the right, before settling my lips against the soft curve of his at the same time that a traitorous tear silently escapes.

On a lightning fast move, Keneth wraps his arms around my waist and lifts me into a - I suppose literal - Bear hug. Squeezing me tight and filling me with all of the love that I don't doubt that he has for me.

"I love you, honey bee." He shakily says as he puts me back on my feet. "I'll see you soon."

With that last statement he swiftly turns around and stalks away without looking back, but I don't fail to notice him wipe his cheeks in his retreat. My heart hurts at how terribly hard it must be for him to leave me here, in the hands of someone trying to sell me, just to support my decision to help a friend, who technically has only ever done me wrong in his eyes.

With a heavy heart I turn to Anton to get this over with. "Let's go. I'm not going to be more ready than I am now."

The guilt and fear in Anton's gaze is impossible to miss as he stares down at me. "I'm going to have to grab your hands behind your back so that it looks like you're my prisoner." He tells me reluctantly.

I pat his cheek softly, feeling the light stubble against the pads of my fingers. "I figured as much. It's okay, you know. I do this for you without hesitation because you deserve love and happiness and if you can't have that with me then I will help you find it."

Turning his head, he puts his hand over mine and kisses my palm softly before nuzzling into it with his eyes tightly squeezed. "I don't deserve a friend like you, and I certainly don't deserve you as anything more than that." Opening his glassy eyes, he kisses my palm again and places my hand on his heart. "No matter what happens, or how long it is before I see you again, you are now and will forever be in my heart, my sweets."

I smile at him through my building tears. How am I meant to get through this when they keep making me cry?

"Right." I croak through my emotions before clearing my throat. "Let's go." I turn around and give him my hands at my back and he takes them gently before guiding me back into the melay.

* * *

APPROACHING a stage built at the end of a tall stone building, I take in the vast amount of male spectators filling the void below, easily over a hundred of them, maybe even two hundred or more.

My heart begins to pitter-patter a little faster at the sight, the possibility of being bought by one of the masses a terrifying thought.

We move down to the side of the building, avoiding the majority of potential buyers in the process, reaching large wooden double doors with ornate knockers stationed in the centre of both.

Reaching up, Anton grabs one, banging it hard three times, still pretending to subdue me with the other hand that is actually tenderly stroking my palm from behind, trying to reassure me, I think.

After a moment the large doors creak open and a man of Asian descent and a long black braid steps through, immediately taking in my presence and looking me up and down with distaste. "A bit late aren't you, Anton?" He sneers, gazing at my pretend captor.

Anton lets out a cold laugh playing the part well, "Does that mean I get to keep her then, Sora?" He asks with a side smirk.

"Not if you want to get paid." Sora snaps, reaching out to grab my arm but Anton pulls me back.

"Hey, hey, hey. Not so fast." Anton coos. "I've earned at least one good squeeze of this fine ass before I hand her over."

Without waiting for a response, he slams me front first into the wall next to the door and grabs at my hips and ass, while he puts his lips to my ear away from Sora.

"Be safe and be careful. I'm so sorry." He whispers in my ear and lightly nips at my lobe. With a sneaky kiss to my cheek he pushes off me and says for production value, "Shame I couldn't fuck you pet."

Sora grabs my arm and pulls me roughly into the doorway.

"Follow me, Anton, I'll take you to the Sorcerer. You're lucky after that stunt, stupid shit."

Pulling me down the hallway, his grip fierce and punishing on my tender flesh making me cry out in pain, we walk fast, Anton hot at our heels. We stop in front of an open door and Sora gestures for Anton to go inside while dragging me away. I glance back before we round a corner to see Anton staring at us, leaning heavily against the wall, looking like he's going to be sick.

Down another hall and a flight of steep stairs we descend until we reach what's clearly a dungeon of some kind. Steel bars lining the pathway to filled cells of women, about ten or so if I guess correctly.

Sora pushes me into the last cell with an open door. I get shoved in with such force that I almost topple over, able to catch myself at the last second.

I go straight to the back wall and place my hands flat on it, concentrating on my heavy breathing, trying to slow down my racing erratic heartbeat.

Calm down. Calm down. The mantra I tell myself over and over again while I focus on breathing in and out slowly, effectively catching my wayward breath.

"Janice?" A voice softly squeaks to my left, and I raise my head at the familiar quiet voice.

"Havana!" I shout unceremoniously and run to the bars she's leaning on, putting my arms through them and holding her close the best I can. "Oh my gosh, I was so worried about you. Are you okay?" I lean back and try to look her over for any obvious injury.

She looked haggard and tired, her beautiful hair a large bird's nest, her skin sallow and grey, her cheeks somewhat hollow since the last time I saw her, and the smell and state of her clothes vile and hard not to flinch away from.

"What happened to you?" I gasp, tears pricking my eyes once more.

Havana just looks down and doesn't answer me, her tiny body trembling in fear. I pull her in for another close hug and rub her back up and down in soft smooth movements hoping to bring her some much-needed comfort.

"It's okay darlin', I'm here and somehow I'll figure something out, but you're not alone anymore." I smooth her hair and feel her shoulders shake as she silently weeps.

We stay like that for a little while before heavy footsteps descend the stairwell and a large bald milky coloured man opens the first cell, forcefully grabbing it's screaming occupant.

The shrill screams echo through the dingy space, reverberating off the stone walls. "Nooo, please, nooo!"

I bang on the bars crying for him to leave her alone, and let her go. Some of the jailed girls join me, while a few just push themselves against the wall and cry, including poor, terrified, Havana.

Nothing helps and the big man just hauls her up the steps against her will, the memory of her screams the only thing left in her wake.

Good gosh. How am I supposed to stop them from taking Havana? The fear I had for myself is now morphing into fear for her because deep down I know I'm going to be okay, but I have no idea how to save my friend.

CHAPTER TWENTY-EIGHT

Anton

My stomach drops as I regretfully watch Janice disappear around the corner, every inch of my body tense and ready to leap after her. What kind of vile creature am I, that I'd do this to a female? What would my own Mother and Father think of me if they saw me now?

I have done some atrocious things in my life cycle but this is by far my worst and biggest mistake. I know it as sure as I know that I'm not worthy of this female. The jealousy I feel towards Keneth roars alive inside of me again, the burning hatred for myself sears into my very core. How nice it must be to be a self-righteous prick that deserves all the special things that life can offer. I wish I could despise him for taking what I desire, what I long for, what I don't know how to live without now that I have *felt* her, *tasted* her, and Celestials strike me down, *love* her. But I can't because he has been more of a friend to me in these last weeks, than I have ever known in my devastatingly long and lonely life. If anyone is worthy of such a beauty, I know it's him, and I have no doubt that he'll protect her with his life.

I turn into the Sorcerers room to wait for him, sitting on the plain, uncomfortable, wooden chair provided with a heavy plonk, donating the defeat I feel strumming through my very bones. Hopefully he won't be too long because I want to get this fucking awful shit over with so that I can get the fuck out of here. As far away from what I've done as I can.

The echo of heavily booted footsteps reach up the hall behind me, the sound of my approaching fate and my heavy heart skips a beat in a mixture of apprehension and guilt. As the male whom the steps belong to nears the room, I regain my self-control and pull my shit together. I have a reputation to uphold after all and I refuse to show weakness. Not only now, but ever, if I can help it.

"Anton, I presume." A lilting, surprisingly soft males voice starts as he enters the room, but I remain facing forward toward the desk, my face hard with a scowl placed for effect.

With a resigned huff, the male continues around me and to his seat behind the desk, talking as he does. "If that's the way you want to do this, it's fine by me."

He's wearing nothing more than low rising leather pants and an open sleeveless black leather hooded vest, covering the top of his long black dreadlocks that hang loosely over his athletic shoulders. His dark oak skin shining with a thin layer of sweat, giving me the assumption that he'd been working out before coming to meet with me.

With eyes as dark as night, he stares unnervingly into my own as he pulls his chair forward, clasping his hands together and leaning his forearms onto his desk.

Making it clear with the ensuing silence that he's done

speaking, I get to the point without so much as a greeting. "I'm owed a wish."

I sit back crossing my ankle over my other leg, placing my hands in my lap and lean back into my chair, waiting for his response. I don't like to waste words on the best of days, and today I sure as shit don't have time for it.

"So I heard." Is all he replies before he taps his hands on the table suddenly on a drum beat. "We'd better get to work then."

Pushing his chair back slightly with a loud screech, he fumbles through his desk drawer before pulling out a piece of paper that looks like a legal document and scrounges around again producing a pen.

"I hope it's worth it." I hear him mumble under his breath as he closes his desk drawer again in a hard thud.

That got my attention. "What the fuck did you say?" My scowl deepens and I grind my teeth.

Waving his hand in dismissal he chimes, "It doesn't matter."

"Like hell it doesn't! If you have something you want to say to me, you'd better say it to my face, Sorcerer." My foot drops down with a bang and I lean forward with my elbows on my knees, ready to pounce if this fuck knob gives me any lip.

"Alright," he says nonplussed by my aggressive attitude, "I said, I hope it's worth it."

"What are you bloody talking about? My wish? It had better be." I growl in confusion.

His eyebrow pops up. "Testy much?" He flicks his hood off and leans back in his chair, looking like he doesn't have a care in the world. "All I'm saying is, that I hope you want something life changing if you've cashed in somebody else's life and freedom for it. It would be one hell of a waste otherwise."

I clear my throat, uncomfortable with his questioning, but I did ask for it. "Since when do you care? You're the one giving wishes away for their lives?"

"Perhaps, Anton, I'm not quite as excited about it as one might imagine." He replies and reaches up to rub at his eyebrows, looking tired all of a sudden. "Not everyone's here because they want to be. Now we're digressing, let's start this again shall we. I'm Twist and I'll be your Sorcerer for the exchange. Do you have any questions regarding how this works or are you happy to just state your desires and be on your way?" His voice is now automated and monotone, with clearly zero fucks to give.

"Whatever, let's get on with it! I'm over this shit and I wanna get out of here." I snap back.

He just stares at me with his eyebrows raised, pissing me off even more.

Growling, I ask fully out of patience now, "What?"

"I'm waiting, numb nuts. What's your wish?" He shakes his head like I'm stupid and mumbles under his breath, "It's not rocket science."

Here it goes. "I wish for one of the ensuing Bear cubs to be my Kindred." I blurt out, unintentionally holding my breath.

With a small smile he scoffs. "I suppose as far as wishes goes, that's a decent one." Getting up in a fluid movement, Twist rounds the table and I stand straight away. I won't have a male stand over me.

"What are you doing?" My voice comes out more hesitant than I would have liked.

Twist pats me lightly on the shoulder, with a serene smile. "Do you want the wish or not? Because I'm going to have to touch you, big fella." Taking a deep breath he continues, "Relax, my friend, this won't hurt, unless she's a grade A asshole. Which, truthfully, would serve you right for selling one woman to get another."

I grumble, "It's no more than I deserve."

He cocks his head to the side at that. "Interesting." Is all he says before lifting his hands to the side of my head without touching me.

A red magenta glow pulses and flicks around the corners of my vision and I stare at his face, watching the black of his eyes shimmer with the same shade of red. As he concentrates, his face changes; hardening and eyes darting all around my face as if he's searching for something.

Suddenly, he sucks in a harsh shaky breath, taking me off guard. His once hardening eyes, turning forlorn and glassy. My hackles rise. I don't think that's meant to happen.

Lowering his hands slowly, the light now gone, Twist steps back, looking down and away so as to not meet my eyes. "I'm sorry, Anton, but you need to make another wish."

"What do you mean? That's the only thing I want. The only thing that will ever be worth it." I cry, fear and frustration filling me. *What's happening?* I desperately grab at his open vest, "Fix it. I told you what I want. Now make it happen!"

He just shakes his head, hand carefully rising to clasp my wrist. "You have to make another wish." He finally looks up at me, his eyes emotive and pleading with me. "I'm so sorry, Anton. I really am."

I suck in a breath and stop breathing. This can't be happening. What the fuck is going on? I can't think, like my brain can't grasp at any one thought. My heart pounds hard and heavy in my chest, so hard I can hear it whooshing in my ears, and I'm frozen, totally frozen. In what? Fear?... I don't know.

"Breathe, Anton, you have to breathe." Twist's grasp tightens on my wrist and his other one slaps my shoulder.

I gasp and let him go, stumbling back a few steps, "I- I don't understand." My hands cup my lowered head, squeezing at it.

Trying to find a reason. "Why?" My normally strong voice, no more than a quiver.

Twist steps forward and puts his arm around my shoulder, guiding me back to the chair. "Sit, my friend. It'll be alright. There must be something else that you want? Perhaps I can hold it as an IOU for now and you can reach me at a later date when you're ready."

I shakily sit down, reduced from the male I was into the nothing I am now. "Shit." I would never have handed her in if I knew this would happen. Why did he look so confident before? Shouldn't he have known if this was beyond him to deliver?

"Is there someone else that I can ask?" My head snaps up and I look at Twist hopefully. "You must know someone who can do this?"

With a groan, his ass leans against the desk behind him. "Mate, no one can help you. What you're asking is impossible."

I shake my head animatedly, "No. I don't accept that. You thought you could do it before, I saw it in your eyes. What changed?" I can't help my mind flashing to Janice locked in a cell, helpless and afraid because of him.

"It's not that it's a hard wish to grant, it's just one that *you* can't have." He says cryptically, looking away from me.

"Do you have *any* idea of what I had to do to get here? To see you?" I yell, leaning forward. "Why me? Am I that broken?" I should have known that the Fates would never gift me a Kindred. I would never deserve one, especially now.

"Ah, shit." I look up at Twist's curse, feeling utterly dejected. "It's not that you aren't worthy, friend, it's just..." He teeters off before finishing.

I rub at my bald scalp, "Just tell me." My tone is hollow, like my chest.

"I can't. I'd love to, but I can't." He sighs. "There's no way I'll get away with it and I'm not willing to throw my life away for someone stupid enough to..." Huffing he pulls away from the desk edge and walks around to his seat, no longer looking as unaffected by the situation as he once seemed.

Walking over, I lean my hands on his desk looking down at his hunched form. "Stupid enough to what?"

Twist pulls at his long dreads, chewing on the side of his hip in thought. "I can't believe I'm going to do this." He moans. "This had better not come back to me saying one damn word, do you understand? If I tell you this, we're square and I don't owe you shit because I can get in a lot of bloody trouble." He narrows his eyes at me.

Anticipation fills me, and a hope that something he tells me will be worth what I've done. I flinch at the memory, sickened by it. "Deal."

"You already have a Kindred. I can't gift you a future one because males can only ever have one." He says, looking directly at me, with something else glinting in his eyes.

How can that be? There are no Bear cubs yet that I know of. I squint at him in suspicion, "Is there more to this you aren't telling me? No Bear females are around yet."

With a boisterous laugh, Twist bends over in his chair, his hand banging on the table in effect. "Are you seriously that stupid?" He huffs out between laughs.

Affronted I say, "What the fuck?"

Twist calms himself down, shaking his head as his dreads flop around, looking at me with... pity? "You're right. You don't deserve her." His voice sounding incredulous.

Janice. She pops into my head like a beautiful dream and I feel myself drain of all colour. "She's- she's my- kindred?" I almost can't get it out, feeling like I'm choking on every painful word.

"You got it, genius." He winks. "Why you were fighting it, is beyond me. You've got to be the dumbest male I've ever come across. You literally sold your Kindred to reproductive slavery so that you could have a Kindred." Eyes wide at me, he flings his hands in the air. "Sucks to be you, my friend."

My stomach drops and I run to grab the trash can next to his desk and vomit the contents of my breakfast in it. Heaving and heaving on my knees until there's nothing left inside me but hurt. *What have I done?*

I hear a voice behind me, "Are you just gonna sit there or are you gonna do something about this?"

His words snap me to action and I run out of the room as fast as I can. Not even leaving a 'Thanks' in my wake. All I know is: I have to find Keneth.

* * *

Outside in the bevie of males clamouring around the stage and floor below, I squish and push my way through the masses, gaze searching for any sign of Keneth.

It takes ten minutes before I spot him standing in a group of formidable males.

"Keneth!" I yell as loud as I can, somehow catching his attention on the first try.

He turns in my direction, and his face pales with worry as he spots me racing towards him. Obviously fearing for our Kindred's safety.

Messaging to the others to follow him, he meets me halfway. "What's happened? Is she okay? What's going on?" He rapidly fires at me.

"She's mine." I cry, eyes wide.

His face softens and he smiles sadly. "I know. I told you that a million times." Keneth's voice is soft but not condescending and I appreciate it.

I grab his shirt, "We have to get her out."

"I take it that this is Anton." A gruff angry voice pulls my attention away. I take in a breath to determine his scent and the moment it hits me, I stiffen. Fear trickles down my spine. There's not that many males that I would have such a reaction for. This is Blayze; the dreaded Phoenix.

"Sir." I bow my head in respect, hoping to the Celestials that I live through this long enough to apologise to Janice.

"So you thought you could take my Kindred's friends, members of my pack and I wouldn't come for you?" He asks me stonily, chestnut eyes hard as granite. Honestly, I didn't think he would, apparently I was wrong.

The fear for Janice's safety overrides my own and I meet his gaze head on. "No, Sir, I did not and I'm sorry for every second that I played a part in it. Janice is my Kindred and I will do anything I can to get her back." My spine strong, I stand to my full height ready to meet any punishment that he may deem fit. "Let me help retrieve her and see her again before you kill me. Please, that's all I ask. I owe her an apology."

Blayze even towers over me, he's so imposing. Yet, he just looks at me as though I didn't just push my luck big time.

His eyebrow slowly arches, "The only reason I haven't killed you yet is because if Summer finds out I did it without Janice's consent, she'll skin me alive and there's no way I'm upsetting that woman. She's living on limited sleep right now. Mina and Demetrius are ravenous." Blayze goes off on a little rant. Apparently Summer's not the only tired one, I note as he yawns deeply.

Keneth claps his hands. "I hate to interfere, but there's a

female coming out. They've started and we need to get Janice out now."

The crowd around us goes wild with howling and hooting as a small female gets dragged screaming out onto the stage.

Turning our heads in disgust by what's happening, we head further away from the crowd.

"Keneth, you're coming with me. I'll need you in order to convince Leon that Janice is claimed." Blayze grabs his arm and begins to move away.

I panic. "What about me?" I yell, following them.

Blayze turns with a frown. "Stay here, Bear. You aren't claimed by her, therefore you are useless to me and will only get in the way. Wait by the saloon entrance and we will bring her out. Let me be clear, this is an order and you better fucking listen."

I feel the air around me heat exponentially at his words, literally. I nod my defeat and watch them walk toward the side door before they disappear inside leaving me filled with apprehension and regret.

CHAPTER TWENTY-NINE

Two more girls have been taken from the first rows of cells, and I'm sick to my stomach. Poor, innocent, Havana, a mere ball in the corner of her cage, looking broken and fragile. Try as I may, I barely get through to her.

Footsteps sound off again at the top of the stairs, this time more than one, making me tense even more. *What if they're taking more of us?* My belief in being saved dwindles with every woman taken.

The faint sound of males quietly chatting joins the heavy stead of their feet, and I try desperately to hear what they're saying as I lean my body as hard as I can against the cold steel bars, my ear facing outward and eyes closed.

They suddenly stop walking and as silence greets me I pop my eyes open, trying to figure out why it just got quiet.

"She's in the last one. Here's the key, get her out and her only." The gruff voice of our guard speaks.

The footfalls turn into the sound of someone running and Keneth comes into view, heading straight for me. "Chuckles?" I breathe out in relief.

His wide grin greets me. "Honey bee, you didn't doubt me did you?" He asks but the emotion in his eyes betrays him. He was worried about me.

Undoing the lock he opens the door and all but rips me out, pulling me tight into his embrace. "Don't ever leave me again." He whispers into my hair.

"Always my saviour, aren't you?" I lean up and kiss him all over his glorious face. "I don't plan to, my love. Never again."

He tries to pull me away but I stop him. "No. We can't leave without Havana." I point down to the small figure in the cage beside my own, looking up at us with the first sign of hope.

"Fuck." I hear a familiar voice snarl. Looking toward the exit, Blayze is standing by the guard, shaking his head. "We need to take her too." He says pointing in her direction and walking to join us.

Havana starts to crawl over towards us until she's gripping the bottom of the bars, staring at Blayze's feet. She never could look any man in the eyes. But it shows a great deal of trust on her part for her to go over to him like that.

Blayze's eyes darken as he takes in her state. Fury evident in their depths. "Why does she look this way?" He demands of the guard.

"They come as they come, buddy. I just guard the flock." He smirks, looking down at the feeble creature before him. "And no. You're not taking her. Leon was very clear that you could only have the claimed female and no more. He also warned me that you would try to take more."

Blayze squares up to him. "Do you know who I am?" He growls.

The guard spits on the ground. "Do you think I give a flying fuck?" Snatching his keys back off Keneth he orders. "Now get out before I call Leon."

Blayze focuses on his breathing, trying to calm down, but I see resignation in his eyes. He can't leave her here.

Havana's hand flies out and snatches the bottom of Blayze's pants with an audible whimper, and he looks down at her with deep regret.

Squatting before her frail form, he says in a soft, gentle tone, "Don't worry, Havana. We won't let anything happen to you. I've brought more gold coins than this place knows what to do with and I can out-bid anyone here." He pauses and sighs, Havana unable to look up from the ground or move. "We will only be gone for a minute, I promise. We'll be right outside and will buy you immediately so you don't have to stand up there too long."

She pulls in a sob and it breaks my heart. "I'll be there too, darlin', and we can go back home together, okay?" I say to her and stroke her outstretched arm softly.

Blayze carefully removes her hand from the bottom of his pants. "I need you to be brave, female. It might seem scary when they come to get you but don't fight it and they won't hurt you." He tries to prepare her. "You will be taken on to a stage and there will be a lot of males there making loud sounds, just don't listen and focus on the floor like you're doing now. I'll pay for you and then you will be free and we can all go home. It's that simple. Can you do that for me?"

Havana nods, still looking down.

I squeeze her hand one more time. "You've got this and we've got you. I'll see you out there." I say with a fake smile.

I hold in a flood of tears threatening to escape as I try desperately to be brave for her. My chest feels tight, as my emotions ravage me.

Keneth pulls me up and puts me under his arm. "Let's go, honey bee, there's some other stuff that we need to talk about."

I nod and let him lead me out, the whole time I look back at my dear friend, hating that I'm leaving her behind, even if it's just for a minute.

Blayze leads us all the way out, without any interference from anybody and I can't help the sigh of relief that escapes me when the fresh breeze caresses my cheek, and the smell of fresh baked bread floats through the air, reminding my stomach of how hungry I am and making my mouth salivate.

"I'm going to join the rest of the team and let them know what's going on. Hermes is holding all the coins, so I need to make sure he's on stand by." Blayze states looking at Keneth with an expression I can't work out. "I believe you have somewhere else to go first?"

I frown at that. *Where else would we have to go?*

Nodding, Keneth grabs my hand and starts to pull me away from the crowd. I try to pull free and ask him where we're going but he's relentless in his pursuit of goodness knows what.

I realise we're headed to the saloon and I'm about to snap at him for going to get a drink when I need to be there for my friend when I spot Anton leaning against the wall, rubbing his shiny head like a genie's about to pop out of it.

"Anton?" I ask bewildered, as we approach.

He snaps to attention, standing up straight as a board. His whole face relaxes in relief before it morphs into one of severe pain.

I let go of Keneth and go to him. "Are you okay?" I ask, touching his stubbled cheek, furrowing my forehead in worry.

Grabbing my hand, he shocks me by dropping to his knees at my feet, kissing every one of my fingers as he looks up at me like I'm the moon in a sea of darkness.

Who is this person and what has he done with Grizzly?

Dropping my hands he bends at the waist and places his head

on my feet. I'm frozen, absolutely frozen. I have no idea what I'm supposed to do with this. Is he broken?

"What are you doing?" I ask quietly, bending over.

He wraps his hands around my calves and murmurs, "I'm sorry."

"Why are you apologising? This was my idea in the end after all." I giggle at how weird he's being.

Sitting back up he looks at me, and Lordy, his cheeks are wet with tears.

"Oh my gosh." I kneel in front of him in front of the saloon, as Keneth watches silently, so that we're level. "Come on now, this is too much. Did you get your Kindred at least?' I ask, wiping a new stray tear.

He takes the side of my face in his hands and nods silently.

"Well, that's great." I lie, because that sucks. I'm regrettably a selfish girl, and I don't want him to be anybody's but mine. My heart sinks even as I plank a tight smile on my lips. "Did he say how long you're gonna have to wait to get her?"

Anton just sits there, boring into my eyes with his, my face cradled in his hands embrace.

"Well?" I ask, needing to know how long I can have with him around before he's gone for good, and trying not to cry.

He licks his lips before asking, "Are you so keen to see me gone?"

My eyes start to defy me and fill with unshed tears. I try to jerk my head away so that he can't see them but he holds me too tight, forcing me to be present. A lone wet traitor glides down my cheek and instead of seeing his judgement, he smiles at me. The kind of smile that makes your heart pitter-patter and the whole room light up.

"Do you want me, sweets?" His baritone voice gets a husky edge and he leans in closer and gently licks the tear from my jaw.

"Souvenir." He whispers moving to my ear and I involuntarily shudder.

Breathing heavy now I choose to be honest, "I will always want you, Grizzly, but I'll always respect your choice to not want me back." My voice hitches at the end with the painful admission.

Pulling back and looking in my eyes with his smile still intact he speaks words I'll never forget. "Sweets, *you* are my Kindred. You're the Kindred I will never deserve, always look up to, never take for granted again and never be able to repay. I promise you, I will follow you anywhere, and spend every day for the rest of our lives becoming a better man for you. I will love you forever, with or without your permission, but I pray to all the Gods that you'll give me another chance."

A sob rips from my throat and I physically tremble, unable to say a word.

"Will you have me, sweets?" He asks quietly now, the smile slipping off his face showing his vulnerability at this moment.

Thrusting myself forward, I land on him with a hard thump, and we unceremoniously tumble onto the dirty floor, with me straddling above him. Grabbing his face, I kiss him hard, with a passion that burns inside me like an eternal flame when it comes to my males.

He returns my kiss with a hungry fervor, grabbing and groping me everywhere he can, as I taste him and get lost in his embrace.

"Um... guys..." Someone says, "Maybe we can do this a bit later?" Shoot, it's Keneth.

Pulling myself away, I look around and realise we've made quite a scene and have gathered a bit of a crowd. Keneth smirks when my face burns hot.

Reaching down he takes my hands and lifts me off a panting Anton. "How about we see to Havana first and then we'll get a room?" He asks politely, trying to hide his obvious amusement.

Fixing my oversized overalls I nod shyly, turning to see Anton already up, with a huge smile and an even bigger hard on. *Oops.*

* * *

HEADING over to the stage area with my Kindreds, we join a fairly large group led by Blayze.

He's not the only familiar face here either. There's a few wolves from my pack, a couple of Bears from Keneth's pack, and even a couple of shifters from Threshold. I recognise the cook in particular; Hermes.

"Hey, Hermes." I greet him with a quick hug that makes my Kindreds grumble. They'll have to get over that, I'm a hugger.

Hermes smiles joyfully at me and with truly genuine words tells me how grateful he is that I'm alive and well.

I've always liked him. Apparently he's meant to be a scary Dragon but I don't see it. He's gentler than a teddy bear despite his mountainous size. He looks like a Viking with his beard and braids down his back.

Deciding to focus on the task ahead I put my full attention into what's going on, not wanting to miss anything in case something important happens.

Sitting through the sale of women was the hardest thing I've ever had to endure. I can't even begin to imagine what it would be like for those that are getting sold. What kind of people would do this? Other than saving them like we are, of course.

Woman after woman, they come and go, testing the limits of my sanity. Knowing that there is nothing I can do but vowing that I will find them and help them somehow.

Suddenly, I understand Summer's intense desire to save people because I would do almost anything to save these women.

What is it that Edmund Burke used to say? 'All that is required for evil to triumph is for good men to do nothing.' And by golly, I will not stand by and watch this happen. We need to bring Leon, and his corrupt system, down.

The crowd slowly starts to disperse as we wait, somewhat impatiently, for Havana to come out. At first, I think it's good because there's less people here now to try to buy her, but eventually the feeling turns to nervousness as time ticks on without any sign of my friend.

Moving forward to the stage's edge, I gaze around at everybody leaving. *What's going on?*

I turn to our group, terror seizing me. My voice is small and shaky. I ask, "Where's Havana?"

EPILOGUE

Havana

PLEASE. *Please. Please.*

My thoughts are naught but pleas for mercy. My body is a trembling heap, stomach empty for days, with no energy to do anything but rock in a ball and pray for sleep to take me.

Janice told me she's coming back. I have to trust her; I have to hold on to that. I refuse to think of anything other than me going to her. I just want to go home. *Please, let me go home.*

Heavy footsteps boom down the stairs, and I brace myself. My fear is spiking so high and hard that I see stars, so I squeeze my eyes shut and just rock. Back and forth. Back and forth. Back and forth.

Why are there two people walking around?

I purposely breathe, trying not to panic as the footsteps pass the other girls and stop in front of my cage.

I have to remember what Blayze said. They will take me outside, and I need to ignore all the *men*. I shudder at the word. *Don't think about it.*

"So..." a smooth voice I've never heard before starts. "This is the female Blayze hopes to rescue, is it? This dirty little thing? Interesting." He's talking about me. *Oh God, why is he talking about me?*

A menacing laugh from the usual guard has me tensing up. "Yep, that piece of crap. Of all the females, *that's* the one they're waiting for."

No. This doesn't sound good. *Please, go away.*

With an impatient sigh, the new man says, "Alright, I'll take her. If he wants her, then I'm happy to ruin his plans. Smug fuck."

Wait. No. I start to rock harder as I hear the cage door unlock and squeak open.

Clomp. Clomp. Clomp.

Someone approaches me, but I'm too scared to open my eyes and just keep rocking. Back and forth. Back and forth.

"Open your eyes, pet," he demands, from too close to me. He must be squatting. "Now!" he shouts so loud my eyes snap open, and I clamber away with my back against the cold, smooth wall.

I quickly look at him and away. I can't bear to see men looking at me, I just can't bear it. *Stop it, stop it.*

"She never looks up at anyone, and I've never heard her utter a word, Sir. I think she might be slow. She doesn't even scream," the guard grunts with a laugh. "You sure you want that one?"

Leaning to the side to take me in more, he says with amusement, "She's not dumb. She's just smart enough to know that she *should* be scared. I can work with that, if anything, I prefer it. I'll have fun breaking this one down even more, and trust me, *I* can make her scream."

He reaches over and grabs my chin roughly as I shake all over so badly that my teeth chatter, forcing my face in his direction. "Listen to me, pet; I am Leon, and now you are *mine*."

ACKNOWLEDGMENTS

A big thank you to my hubby, wife, and spawn of my loins. Your love means more to me than anything else in the world. There are no words that will ever be good enough to express my love for you.

Thank you to my family and friends for always having my back and supporting me in all of my endeavours. It's very appreciated.

I have been lucky enough in this business to also make some amazing friends in the book community that inspire me to always better myself and have taught me to appreciate every goal I achieve along the way. AJ, Rosie, Kira, Gemma, Liliana, Claire, Eve and all the rest of the amazing babe's; I'm really blessed to know you and consider you a friend.

To my PA's Emma and Kristin, you're everything I never knew I needed. I worship you at your feet, for the magic you make happen.

Branka, Lola, and Bobbi; I miss you guys every day.

Ashleigh and Chelsea, we are in dire need for a catch up. You ladies always give me the feeling of home.

My beta readers, thank you for being the first people to tell me where I've fucked up. You ladies keep me from embarrassing myself. Thank you.

Hmm... I think I forgot someone...

Psych! Amanda, love ya bitch! You are the absolute shit and

stuck with me forever. I am so grateful for every single motha fuckin thing you do. You help me get through all the shit, even when both Brian's have pissed off at the pub.

ABOUT THE AUTHOR

Hi, I'm Alexandra, an Aussie/Kiwi mother of three, married to the best husband around.

My life is surrounded with lots of animals because I just can't say no to all their cuteness. I have a rare chronic illness that keeps me grateful for the beauty that life brings and my pen name is in honour of my amazing Grandparents who are *everything* to me.

My soul lives off coffee, family, reading, storms, good scotch and great wine, mountains, and is a real knowledge whore.

I'm a firm believer in being kind to others because it *does* matter, and it *does* make a difference. If I can make just one person happy with my stories or even to give them a reprieve they may desperately need to escape their harder reality, then I've done my job right.

My imagination is a constantly growing paradise for me and I feel blessed that I get to share a little of it with you.

Thank you for coming on my journey with me; You *are* appreciated.

If you have enjoyed my story, please take the time to leave me a review on amazon. Reviews are the bread and butter of indy authors and every one counts.

Here are some links to my social media accounts:

Facebook Group:

https://www.facebook.com/groups/alexandrasguardians

Facebook Page:

https://www.facebook.com/Alexandra.K.Martin.Books

Amazon:

https://www.amazon.com/Alexandra-K-Martin/e/B08NHK4JC4/

Instagram:

https://instagram.com/alexandra.k.martin.books?igshid=1m508hfimy8zz

Goodreads:

https://www.goodreads.com/author/show/20962962.Alexandra_K_Martin

Newsletter

https://mailchi.mp/27cd881447ed/alexandrakm-nl

Tiktok:

https://vm.tiktok.com/ZSeM3U4HQ/

Website to come…

OTHER BOOKS BY ALEXANDRA K. MARTIN

Series

Rathe Chronicles (Epic Fantasy Romance)

-Summer's Confine, Book One (RH)

-Janice's Entanglement, Book Two (Menage)

-Havana's Hell, Book Three (MF)

-Alice's Coalition, Book Four (RH)(Coming 2022)

Standalones

-Broken Faun (Paranormal RH/ Coming Mar 2022)

Collaboration/Standalone

-Lust: A Golden Bird Retelling. Sinners Fairytales Collaboration, Book Six (Dark Contemporary RH)

Anthologies

-Hidden Fate (RH), featured in 'Rebirth of the Dark Hunter' (Urban Fantasy/ Coming Feb 2022)

-Dom X (MF), featured in 'My Perfect Pleasure' (Erotic/ Coming May 2022) CO-WRITE as SOULSISTERS

A SINNERS FAIRYTALE COLLABORATION; LUST

Link to the Pre-Order: https://books2read.com/Lustsins

www.ingramcontent.com/pod-product-compliance
Lightning Source LLC
Chambersburg PA
CBHW030411310726
48979CB00002B/367

* 9 7 8 0 9 7 5 6 2 5 5 3 8 *